A big hello from me to you. . .

. . . and hope you're ready for another mooch around the slightly strange world of Sadie Bird. Her twin brother Sonny is still aiming for stardom (in a very dubious stage outfit), and her friend Cormac is still aiming to be a top stand-up comedian (but keeping his job as, er, a trainee undertaker).

Be prepared for a surprise (and shock) or two, plus the appearance of quite possibly the most horrible little brother ever. (If you have one like Harry, I feel truly, truly sorry for you. . .)

Macho love

Karen McCombie

KAREN McCOMBIE

SCHOLASTIC

For Betty L.
"For warmest thoughts and wishes,
to travel where you are."

Scholastic Children's Books
An imprint of Scholastic Ltd
Euston House, 24 Eversholt Street
London, NW1 1DB, UK
Registered office: Westfield Road, Southam, Warwickshire, CV47 0RA
SCHOLASTIC and associated logos are trademarks and or registered
trademarks of Scholastic Inc.

First published in the UK by Scholastic Children's Books, 2008

Text copyright © Karen McCombie, 2008
The right of Karen McCombie to be identified as the author of this work has
been asserted by her.

Cover illustration copyright © Rian Hughes, 2008

10 digit ISBN 978 1407 10502 4
13 digit ISBN 1 407 10502 7

Typeset by M Rules
Printed by CPI Bookmarque, Croydon, Surrey
Papers used by Scholastic Children's Books are made
from wood grown in sustainable forests.

1 3 5 7 9 10 8 6 4 2

www.scholastic.co.uk/zone

Contents

Dog, the cat bundle

Deep joy.

I was suffering from the exact *opposite* of it.

Usually the only way to cheer myself up at joy-less moments is to go and listen to very loud, very fast music and dance round my room (door firmly closed) like a maniac. It's very medicinal, y'know.

The Foo Fighters would've been my ideal choice this Saturday morning, but I was pretty sure Dad had taken their CDs when he moved out of his Bachelor Pad and into the Flat of Gloom, and I hadn't got any of their stuff on my iPod. So instead, I'd come outside to visit my pet Christmas tree.

With the faint waft of sick in the air and Dog in my arms, I settled myself down on the spongy, pine-needled undergrowth and *sighhhhhhed. . .*

Hmmm, maybe I should explain stuff quickly, in reverse order:

- Dog is my cat
- The sick smell was baby barf (my sister, Martha's), which I thought I'd cleaned off my top, but obviously hadn't completely
- The Christmas tree is planted in a mini-wood between the end of my garden and the start of the cemetery that our house backs on to
- Until four weeks ago, Dad lived in the room above our garage, but had moved into a flat, above (wait for it) an undertaker's. (Yes, I know there seem to be a lot of dead people in my world. But I'm really not that morbid – promise!)
- And the sensation of non-deep joy? That was caused by. . . Well, do you have a comfort-blankie outfit?

No, not an outfit *made* from comfort blankies (that would be *way* too gross). I mean, the sort of thing that you put on when you think you're looking urgh, a bit like Shrek or something, and suddenly you feel all right? Even kind of nice?

My friend Hannah's comfort-blankie outfit is her black Rolling Stones T-shirt, with the Stones' famous sticking-out tongue on it. Whenever she puts it on, she mutates into a v. groovy rock goddess, instead of a thirteen-year-old music-dunce who couldn't hum a Rolling Stones tune if you paid her a hundred quid. My other friend, Letitia, has this really deep-pink, sort of hippy smock top that looks great with her dark skin, and whenever she wears it, it's total, instant *wow*.

My comfort-blankie item of clothing is my skinny black cardie, guaranteed to go with T-shirts, jeans and leggings and stuff (i.e., what I wear most of the time) and dresses up when I'm dressing up – which is like, never.

Correction: my comfort item of clothing *was* my skinny black cardie, etc., etc.

I say "was", 'cause it had just died. Now I'd be stuck looking like Shrek *for ever*. . .

Yeah, yeah, I know I get too dramatic sometimes and, OK, my cardie hadn't *died* exactly, but it wasn't feeling very well. *You* wouldn't feel very well either if you'd been snaggled, barfed on and eaten.

"Why can't you just do the purring bit and leave out the clawing stuff?" I now whispered to Dog, as I cuddled her – or, more accurately, *restrained* her – on my lap with one hand. With the other, I examined the damage: loops of black wool that had been yanked out at boob level.

"Prrrrp?"

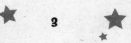

At the sound of my voice, Dog tried and failed to turn her head around. The clear plastic lampshade collar round her neck made it very hard for her to do many things, including chew her leg bandage. It also made it *easy* for her to bump into a variety of things and look slightly stupid, which would be kind of entertaining, if I didn't feel so sorry for her.

So Dog was guilty of the snaggling part but, really, the whole snaggling, barfing, eating disaster was *Sonny's* fault.

It might not seem like it if you looked at the situation, and realized that my twin hadn't been anywhere *near* me when all the snaggling etc. had happened. But if you took your time, and thought about it hard – like I'd just done – it was perfectly logical.

I mean, if my "darling" brother hadn't secretly auditioned for a boy band last month, then he wouldn't have got himself in a state about admitting it to me, in case I thought it was deeply naff and teased him rotten about it (how right he was).

And if Sonny hadn't have got himself in a state, he wouldn't have kicked his ball around the garden in such an uptight way, and ended up booting Dog off the top of the wall with one over-enthusiastic kick.

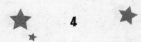

And if he hadn't knocked Dog off the wall, she wouldn't have torn her cruciate ligament (you don't need to know, just think "ouch!"), and been confined to a big cage in the living room for eight weeks till it healed.

And if Dog wasn't stuck inside the stupid cage, then I wouldn't have felt all sorry for her today and crawled in to give her a hug. So *she* wouldn't have clawed her love and happiness on my chest (make that my cardie) to show her gratitude.

With me so far?

And if I hadn't been stuck in the stupid cage, trying to unhook Dog, I might have scrambled to my crying little sister, Martha, in her bouncy chair sooner, i.e. well before she randomly barfed her breakfast all over me. And if I hadn't been sitting cross-legged on the floor afterwards, trying to clean up me, my unfortunate cardie and Martha with baby wipes, Clyde (our house-friendly rabbit) wouldn't have been able to sidle up unseen, and test the corner of my cardie out in case it happened to be a tasty snack. (He ended up eating a peach-sized hole out of it, and a button.)

See? Just like I said: snaggled, barfed on and eaten. Poor cardie.

And like I said, all Sonny's fault, *obviously*.

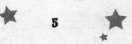

"*No*," I suddenly said sternly, as Dog spied a squirrel hopping around in the old graveyard that we were gazing at from my favourite chill-out spot by the Christmas tree. "You're out here for fresh air *only* – no running off!"

Not that Dog could have got too far with that collar on – she'd bang into every twig and branch going.

"Is it a good idea to take Dog outside?" my sort-of-stepdad, Will, had asked only a few minutes ago. While Mum caught up on a backlog of school marking, Will had been busy putting washing away, and of course *that's* when Martha had bounced, bounced, *bounced* in her chair and then barfed. He'd come back into the living room just in time to pick up the newly-cleaned Martha, leaving me free to shoo Clyde away from my cardie and take Dog out of the cage for a glimpse of daylight in the garden (and beyond).

"She'll be fine!" I'd assured Will, scooping a startled Dog into my arms and heading towards the kitchen and the back door. Of course, Dog *wasn't* fine. The minute she smelled grass and flowers and secret scents on the breeze (not to mention spotting skittering squirrels) she was desperate to be off, wrecked leg or no wrecked leg. And with all that wriggling and restraining, the daisy chain I'd planned to make to accessorize her ugly plastic collar hadn't materialized. I'd only got to two flowery links, which was hardly enough for a daisy *ring*.

Holding on to my wannabe escapee cat with one hand, I shook one arm out of my poorly cardie, swapped hands and did the same on the other side. Quickly, before she could protest, I wrapped Dog up in my cardie-cum-straightjacket. (Hey, it was all it was good for now.)

"There we go! Right – come on, you," I said, getting to my feet and heading back to the house with Dog-the-cat-bundle.

As we ducked through the gap in the old metal railing that separated our garden from the graveyard, a sudden sound made me nearly bump my head.

"Oh, *yeahhhhhhhhhhhhhh!*"

"*Yeahhhhhhhhhhhhhhhhhh, babyyyyy!*"

The noise was a duet, two voices bellowing along together in perfect disharmony. Uh-oh – any neighbours hoping for a Saturday morning lie-in were in trouble.

I straightened up, and me and Dog stared up at the source of the racket: the open window of the bedroom above the garage. The room my dad had

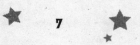

as his Bachelor Pad during the three *looonnnnggggg* years between him splitting up with Mum and *finally* moving out.

Now that room belonged to Sonny.

"Hold it, hold it!" I heard Sonny call out.

His idiot friend Kennedy held it. Or at least went thankfully silent.

"Let's try again!"

"OK!!"

Oh, *no*. Sonny and Kennedy could both sing (darn *right* they could sing; both my parents and Kennedy's had paid out plenty in stage-school fees to teach them to warble). The trouble was, the boys didn't seem to be able to sing *together*.

Excuse me for being cynical, but this didn't bode well for the band they were both in and that was supposed to be signing a record deal sometime in the imminent future (according to Benny, the stage-school lecturer guy who'd got all these "talented young performers" together in the first place).

"Oh, *yeahhhhhhhhhhhhhh!*"

"*Yeahhhhh – uh YEAHHHHHHHHHHH, BABYYYYY!*"

Urgh. Kennedy changing key there didn't really help. Dog's ears bent back against her head in protest. If she hadn't been stuck in a

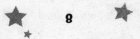

straightjacket, and if she hadn't been wearing a lampshade collar, I bet she'd have clamped her fluffy, tortoiseshell paws over her ears.

"Let's get inside," I muttered to my cat bundle, hurrying towards the back door that led into the kitchen.

And then I looked up; up at the window directly above the open back door. The window with the taste-free Arsenal Football Club curtains that Sonny hadn't got round to taking down and moving to his new room yet (along with piles of programmes for every West End show he'd been to see and several solo socks).

Actually, that gave me an idea. No, not about the socks, exactly. Despite it being bigger than mine, I'd resisted the idea of moving into Sonny's old room up till now 'cause a) I was still huffing a bit that Sonny had automatically been given Dad's Bachelor Pad when Dad had moved out, and b) I didn't really want a hand-me-down from Sonny, even if it was a hand-me-down in the shape of a roomy room. But now I'd changed my mind; it was a lot further away from the Bachelor Pad (and the warbling) than my current bedroom, and that had to be a very good thing indeed. . .

Plopping my ridiculous-looking cat bundle

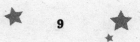

down on the nearest kitchen worktop, I fished my phone out of the back pocket of my jeans.

Fancy a bit of a party at my place later? I keyed in. *Come at 6pm. Dress slobby.*

Ping! – off the texts flew to my two best friends.

Bleep! – off went my phone, so that Hannah and Letitia couldn't phone me back and pester me about what I meant exactly.

Hey, I like a bit of mystery. Though the biggest mystery in my life, of course, was how I came to be related to this dork who'd just walked into the kitchen, all hair-gel spikes and gosh-I'm-handsome! grin.

("The two of you are like . . . like that yin and yang thing; opposites that complement each other!" Gran said all sagely last week when I complained that I had more in common with Clyde, our slightly grouchy rabbit, than my own twin brother.)

"Hey, Sadie!" said Sonny, in his usual, annoyingly chirpy voice. "Me and Kennedy are just running through some songs. Wow, I'm thirsty. Doing vocals this early in the day can really wreck your voice, if you're not careful. That's what all my vocal coaches always warn me. I should've warmed up first, but I got into working on some lyrics that came into my head last night, and I thought I'd better write them down before I forgot them. I was thinking that I'll show them to my tutor Benny later, and see if he thinks they're any good for the band."

Sigh. I'd come into the kitchen for a bit of refuge, and Sonny ends up trotting down for a post-breakfast snack raid on the fridge. We'd somehow, *blissfully*, missed each other over Cheerios this morning.

"How utterly sensational to see you too," I said drily, checking the time on my watch – 9.03 a.m. "What's Kennedy doing here so early?"

There was no chance of the rest of us having a lie-in with Martha around, but Kennedy didn't have a baby sis with the yelling power of an alarm clock.

"He came by to get me – there's a band rehearsal happening this morning," said Sonny, as he made a grab for a two-litre carton of orange juice.

Help. He was opening his mouth again. He was just about to give me a ton of information about this morning's band rehearsal, which I hadn't asked about, and didn't want to know.

"Yeah, today we've got to work on our – hey! What happened to *Dog*?"

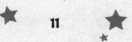

Phew. Sonny had just noticed the cat bundle perched on the kitchen unit and got distracted from his monologue on the amazing life of, well, *him*.

I knew that he meant Dog looked weird, as if that famous modern artist bloke – Damien Hirst, the one who put half a cow in a tank – had tried fusing her with a table lamp in an attempt to win the next Turner Prize or whatever.

"*You* happened to her, remember?" I replied, untangling my cardie quickly, so that a slightly dizzy Dog was left perched on the worktop, wrapping-free apart from her bandage and plastic collar.

No harm in reminding Sonny that he broke our cat, I thought to myself, as I distractedly held up my cardie to inspect the damage once again.

"*Yuck* – is that *puke* on there, Sadie?!"

"Yep," I said, nodding at the dried-in barf stain. "I was listening to you and Kennedy singing and I couldn't stop myself being sick!"

"Very funny," droned Sonny, one eyebrow all arched, as he helped himself to a large handful of Baby Bel cheeses.

"Yes, I am, thank you," I replied. "Can you step on the bin pedal, please?"

"You're just jealous," said Sonny, doing what he

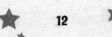

was told and stepping on the pedal, while closing the fridge door with his elbow.

Splat – in went the balled-up dead cardie. A perfect shot on my part.

"Jealous of what?" I said brightly, turning to grab Dog as she began dangerously readying herself for a jump to floor level.

"Me and Kennedy!"

"Well, you *do* make a lovely couple!!" I said, breezing past Sonny and heading towards the living room, as he spluttered and struggled (and failed) to come back with a snappy something in reply.

As I eased Dog back into her metal-caged prison cell and heard Sonny stomping up the stairs, I was surprised to realize I suddenly felt . . . well, if not deep joy, something *like* it.

Hurrah for Sonny. I often wondered what he was good for, and now I knew: teasing him mercilessly had cheered me up no end.

Bless my "darling" brother. . .

Yin, Yang, *yuck*. . .

Paint? Check.

Crisps? Check.

Yep, those were the perfect ingredients for my Saturday night party. Tonight's room-painting party. Oh, yes: later on, with only my gratitude and some Kettle Chips as payment, my unsuspecting friends (suckers!) were going to help me transform a dodgy boy's room into a stunning teen boudoir for me.

And, joy of joys, my lovely not-quite-stepdad, Will – who usefully suffers from a touch of obsessive-compulsive disorder – was right now hoovering the dust mountains and generally disinfecting the room of its boy germs while me and Mum shopped. Fab.

"Oh, *no!*" I suddenly groaned, staring down at the two, large heavy tins of paint at my feet.

"What – did we get the wrong kind? We didn't pick up gloss instead of matt by mistake, did we?"

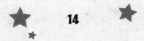

Mum asked in a panic, glancing away from the road and into the passenger-side footwell, where the tins were nestled beside a Sainsbury's bag crammed with crisps. "Do we need to drive back?"

Me and Mum had had a nice time wandering around Homebase together, with Martha in her buggy cooing and drooling, but I didn't think she much fancied doing a U-turn in the busy Saturday lunchtime traffic and paying a return visit there, specially with a newly-napping baby in the back of the car.

"It's not that. . ." I sighed. "It's the colour!"

"But you spent ages choosing it," said Mum, her gaze back on the road, but her forehead set in a concerned frown. "Don't you like it?"

Of course I liked it. That's why I'd taken ages choosing it. It was a light greeny-blue, the sort of pale jewel colour of the sea where it laps close to the shore on the cover of a tropical island holiday brochure.

It was from a paint range where the hook was that they were all supposed to be very soothing shades. (The dusky pink was pretty nice, same for the light, heathery mauve. The pasty browny one wasn't particularly lovely, but then maybe I'm not one of those people who find dried mud very soothing.)

"I love it!" I assured her. "It's just. . . it's just the name of it!"

"What about it?" Mum frowned some more, reaching over to turn down her beloved BBC Radio 3 (classical music, since that's Mum's thing) so that she could properly get to grips with the problem.

And then, of course, I felt pretty stupid and wished I'd kept my mouth shut.

"It's . . . well, the shade is called 'Yin and Yang'," I muttered.

"So?" said Mum, sounding confused, and so she should, I guess. She wasn't to know that Gran had described me and Sonny as being like yin and yang. She wasn't to know that I didn't even properly understand what yin and yang *meant*, only that I didn't like *anything* that linked me and Sonny together.

"It just sounds . . . pretentious," I said, grabbing for a word that hopefully sounded like I knew what I was talking about.

"There's nothing pretentious about yin and yang. It's a very ancient Chinese idea, all about how two opposite things can together be very harmonious," said Mum, suddenly sounding like the teacher she was. Pity her subject was music, and not Rambling Chinese Ancientness. "Haven't you seen the symbol for it?"

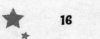

"Nope," I said flatly, resting my feet on the paint pots (but obviously not on the crisps – I didn't want to risk breakages).

"There are two interconnecting shapes – black and white – that make a circle together. They're sometimes characterized by one being female and negative, while the other is male and positive."

How ironic, I thought. *Me and my pet sarkiness, and Sonny and his irritating bouncy pet puppy-ness.*

"It can be a very beautiful way to describe a couple, really," said Mum dreamily, thinking of herself and Will, I was sure, as she pulled over to the pavement in busy Blackstock Road. Right in front of the glossy black frontage of McConnell & Sons, Funeral Directors.

"Hey, Sadie! Hi, Nicky!!"

Mum leant over into the passenger side I'd just got out of, and twisted her head up to see Dad, who was waving enthusiastically down at both of us from the open first-floor window.

She hated being called Nicky.

"Fancy coming up, Nic? You haven't seen the place yet!" Dad called down. In the past month since he'd been living here, his browny-blond sideburns had got longer and his Hawaiian shirts had got louder.

Mum hated being called Nic even more than

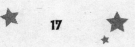

she hated being called Nicky. And she'd never liked Dad growing sideburns, or his taste in loud shirts. I think it's fair to say that my parents' yin and yang inter-connectedness had mouldered away *years* ago.

"Sorry, got stuff to do!" Mum excused herself cheerfully.

She's a bit dippy, my mum, and never seemed to mind my dad's long, slow, extended exit from the house. But now that he was officially gone, I think she was quite enjoying the peace and quiet, i.e. no blaring loud rock music drowning out Elgar or whoever was her composer of the month. (OK, so she still had blaring loud rock music blasting from my room and Sonny's, but at least she could threaten us with no pocket money if we didn't turn it down.).

"Can you stick that stuff up in Sonny's old room for me?" I asked Mum, pointing to the paint and crisp combo in the footwell.

"Sure." She nodded, turning up the radio as some tubas started tubing or whatever they do in classical music. "Have a nice visit. See you later!"

And, in a quick dart of Ford Focus and to the sound of blaring arpeggios (I think that's a musical term, but it might be some kind of pasta), Mum blurred into the busy traffic.

"Hurry up!" Dad grinned down at me on the pavement. "Lunch is ready!"

As soon as Dad pressed the entry buzzer, I pushed open the door next to the undertaker's office and hurriedly stomped up the stairs. I was starving (shopping for crisps is a tempting business, but I'd managed to resist), and Gran's cooking was always excellent. Of course, I still thought it was ridiculous that our gran had moved out of her own roomy bungalow in Barnet and into Dad's tiny box room to "help him settle in", but it was times like this – i.e. when my stomach was rumbling – that I was glad she was there. Otherwise I'd be eating lukewarm Pot Noodle for lunch.

"Hi!" I called out, walking through the front door of Dad's flat, and turning right into the living room.

"Hi!" said a teenage boy who wasn't my brother.

This teenage boy was. . .

a) Sitting on my dad's favourite battered, tan leather chair
b) Dad's upstairs neighbour
c) Called Cormac
d) Seventeen

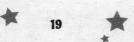

19

e) Wearing a black suit and tie, and

f) Trying very hard not to dribble Pot Noodle on his black suit and tie

Cormac was all right. I hadn't much liked him when I first knew him, I guess 'cause I resented him buddy-ing up with my dad as soon as Dad rented this place from Cormac's father. Though I'd sort of decided by now that it was more a case of Dad semi-adopting Cormac, 'cause he missed talking music, comedy, and other random rubbish with his *real* kids (i.e. me and Sonny).

"So Gran's out, then?" I asked, as Dad came out of the kitchen, holding a plastic pot of semi-softened noodles towards me. Bits of undissolved powdery sauce floated on the top of too much water. How could Dad even get Pot Noodle so badly wrong?

"Mmm, gone down the market." Dad rolled his eyes. "She's threatening to buy a tablecloth!"

A quick glance around showed that Gran's determined pretty-fication of the flat was steam-rolling ahead. For every bit of brushed chrome gear that Dad had bought (think stereos, top-of-the-range recordable DVD players, surround-sound, High Definition-ready TV monitors),

Gran had matched it with a lacy doily or some corny ornament.

"She even tried to put dried flower arrangements on top of both the speakers." Dad laughed.

He'd relegated the dried flowers and their equally flowery vases to either side of the fireplace, I noticed. The fireplace that he was using as a display unit for messy piles of his precious Q and *Mojo* music magazines. (Maybe Gran was going to chuck the tablecloth over them to make a feature for the room?)

"Where's Sonny, then?" I asked, kicking off my Converse trainers (easy to do, since I always wore them as non-official slip-ons, with the heels folded down). I settled myself on the squeaky new black leather sofa.

By the way, just 'cause I was asking about Sonny, don't get me wrong; I wasn't badly missing my twin or anything. I was perfectly happy with just Dad for company – and Cormac. It's just that Sonny and me always came round to Dad's for lunch and a visit on Saturdays.

"He phoned about an hour ago – his rehearsal's running on a bit," said Dad, plonking himself and his own Pot Noodle down beside me on the sofa. He flicked from one music station to another on the TV. "So how're you doing, Sadie?"

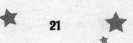

Ah, see? This is why it felt good not to have Sonny around. When Sonny was in a room, he was the one who did eighty per cent of the talking and, whether he meant it or not, got eighty per cent of the attention. There were times when he'd prattle on and endlessly on about whatever song lyrics/dance moves/acting roles he was doing at his dumb old stage school, and I'd find myself sitting very still, directing telepathic messages telling him to, "SHUT UP! SHUT UP! *SHUT UP!*".

It's a great disappointment to my gran that Sonny and me don't have some spooky, psychic link, and at times like that it was a disappointment to me too. . .

"I'm fine," I replied to Dad's question, stirring frantically at my Pot Noodle to make it more edible. "School's been just thrilling. A non-stop, exciting whirl of dull subjects, horrible homework and grumpy teachers."

Dad and Cormac both laughed. They both got my sarcastic sense of humour. Mum was so dippy that my sarcasm just sort of flew over the top of her head, and it just plain confused Sonny.

And actually, I was pretty chuffed that I made Cormac laugh: he was a future stand-up comedian, after all, so if *he* thought I was funny, that was sort of . . . great.

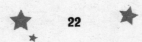

As I swirled congealed noodles, I half-daydreamed to myself that one day in the future, me and Cormac could be this famous comedy duo, getting our own show on Channel 4 or something. Hey, maybe Sonny *wasn't* destined to be the famous one in our family, as everyone – *especially* Sonny – thought.

"How's the comedy stuff going?" I asked Cormac hopefully. It's not like he was exactly big on the comedy circuit of North London yet. His only "performance" so far had been a couple of Sundays ago, standing on a small wooden box in the middle of Highbury Fields park, just along the road.

"Haven't really had much time to think about it lately," said Cormac, raising his red eyebrows up, towards his equally red hair. "Work's been madly busy."

"Right." I nodded, like that was a pretty reasonable explanation. Yeah – till it dawned on me that for Cormac's work to be madly busy, it meant there's been a rush on dead people lately. *Yeww. . .*

"So I've just been doing research mostly, watching more comedy DVDs."

Cormac pointed a dribbling fork towards the ceiling of Dad's flat, in the direction of the place

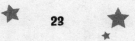

he called home. He was sharing with his big brother, Dad had told me, till building work got finished on his parents' house, somewhere in Stoke Newington. I guess it was handy for Cormac to be staying there in the meantime; it couldn't be any closer to work (all he and his brother had to do was trundle down the green metal fire escape at the back of the building of a morning).

For a second, I tried to imagine what the flat upstairs looked like; plain, gloom-grey walls maybe? A few copies of *Funerals Today* magazine fanned out on the coffee table? Matching black suits hanging up in the wardrobe?

"Sadie – can you get that?" Dad called through from the kitchen.

I shook myself out of my split-second fantasy of the McConnell sons' bleak flat. I hadn't noticed the phone ringing, or Dad getting up to cremate toast.

"Hello?" I said, leaning sideways along the length of the black sofa, balancing the Pot Noodle in one hand and tucking the phone under my chin with the other.

Helpfully, Cormac did a little leaning of his own and turned down the volume of the Police CD playing in the background.

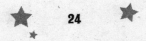

"Hey, Sadie, is Dad there?" an oh-so-familiar voice prattled in my ear.

"Who is this?" I asked my brother.

"*Sonny*, of course!" said Sonny, falling for my wind-up. Oh, it was just too easy sometimes. . .

"So is Dad there?"

"He's busy." Busy burning stuff.

"OK, well then, can you tell Dad I won't be able to make it round this afternoon after all, 'cause rehearsals are still running on, and Benny says we really need to nail these harmonies."

Benny, Benny, Benny. The way Sonny talked about his new teacher made me feel like going and getting him an altar so he could put Benny photos on it and worship him.

"So, you're going to tell Dad, right?" Sonny checked with me, since I hadn't said anything.

"Yep, I'll tell Dad you can't come, 'cause you're busy."

"Tell him we're still rehearsing. Tell him that Benny says he's expecting to hear from the record company on Monday, and tell him it's really exciting 'cause Benny says they might even throw us a party whenever they get us in to sign the con—"

"DADDDDD!" I yelled, holding the phone away from my ears, unable to listen to a second

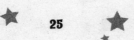

more of Sonny wittering on about his band and his generally exciting life. "IT'S FOR YOU!!!"

I know it might sound like I could be diagnosed as suffering from a bad case of envy, 'cause of Sonny being at stage school and 'cause of him being in some proper, (maybe) chart-bound band – but you'd be absolutely *wrong*.

I mean, I'm realistic. I'm not like those people who audition for TV talent shows, thinking they're destined to be the next global megastar, when really they've got the vocal talent of a guinea pig. I *knew* I was the twin with no discernable singing/dancing/acting talent, so I could hardly expect to be sent to stage school, same as Sonny, could I?

And I wouldn't have blinked an eye at my hyper-talented brother flouncing around in jazz dance classes while I was stuck at the local school doing double history lessons, IF HE WOULD ONLY STOP TALKING ABOUT IT VIRTUALLY EVERY WAKING SECOND OF THE DAY.

"Dad? Dad?" his tinny voice vibrated in my outstretched hand.

"For me?" said Dad, coming out of the kitchen and juggling a burning hot, blackened piece of something that must have once been a

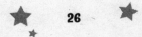

slice of bread between his hands (may it rest in peace).

As I handed him the phone, I glanced over at Cormac, who was quickly flicking through one of Dad's music magazines, nodding his head softly in time to a track I particularly liked called "Every Little Thing She Does Is Magic". He seemed to sense he was being stared at; he gazed up and gave me a shy smile. In that instant, I suddenly wished I had someone ordinary like Cormac as my brother, instead of super-talented, super-show-off Sonny.

And in the next instant, Cormac narrowed his eyes at me, not sure if I was laughing or choking or mad. The answer was: all three.

I mean: Cormac, *ordinary*? I was pretty crazy to think that! What's ordinary about a teenage trainee funeral director who wants to be a stand-up comedian?

It was too funny, really, though I immediately realized it's best *not* to start laughing at something that pops in your head when you've got a mouthful of semi-congealed noodles. . .

Deep, dark sarcasm

Suckers.

Hannah and Letitia (bless 'em) had turned up, as invited, for the "party" at my house.

Luckily for me, both my best friends liked me very much (who knows *why*), and didn't hold it against me that I'd basically conned them into painting Sonny's old bedroom.

Unfortunately, neither of them had bothered taking any notice of the bit of my text that had said "dress slobby", and both arrived in their regulation not-trying-too-hard-but-looking-pretty-good best outfits. (Hannah in white jeans, gold belt and an AC/DC band T-shirt, Letitia in skinny-rib, fuchsia-pink vest top, crop jeans and new cornrows).

They needed painting gear, and since we didn't have a cupboard full of handy overalls, I'd improvized with a crushed bundle of old pyjamas I'd found at the back of my bottom drawer when

I was sorting stuff out for my room move. Hannah was in polka-dot flannel PJs, Letty had on a Lisa Simpson nightshirt, and I'd joined them by pulling on a pair of pristine, never-worn pink pyjamas with a "cute" teddy on the front. (Thanks, Auntie Diane. Hope you don't object to the fact that I've customized Mr Teddy with glasses and a beard and moustache drawn on in blue biro. . .)

I'd commemorated the moment on my camera, of course. Hopefully, none of us would dressed this dumb again.

Fat chance.

"Bet you'd look good with your head green. . ."

That was Hannah, singing along to the Arctic Monkeys' "Bet You Look Good On The Dancefloor" (one of me and Dad and Sonny's favourite ever singles), only adapting the lyrics slightly.

The "you" she was referring to was her brother, Harry, and the "green" was inspired by the colour of paint she was splashing on my (new) bedroom wall.

She'd already taken a long, musing look at the open paint-pot, trying to figure out if a ten-year-old's head would fit in there, if pushed.

Harry. Now there's a cute little brother to

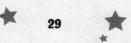

29

have – if you're *insane*. It was kind of hard for Hannah to think warmly of a sibling who'd dedicated his ten-year-old life so far to playing practical jokes on her (and her friends, I remembered with horror, thinking of the dreaded toilet and cling film incident).

"Hey, what was the *first* stunt Harry ever pulled on you?" I asked Hannah, as I dipped my roller in the paint tray.

His most *recent* was the "I SMELL" sign he'd stuck on her back as she'd left home earlier. It wouldn't have been so bad if Hannah'd only walked from her house (Number 50) to mine (Number 135), but sadly for her, she'd taken a detour to the shop to buy a carton of juice and some crisps to bring round, going via a bus stop and a packed fish and chip shop queue. *Not* good.

"He was two," said Hannah, matter-of-factly. Which made her five years old at the time.

"*That* young?" said Letitia in surprise, adjusting the shower cap on her head, to make sure it was properly protecting her all-new cornrows from green paint splatters. The thing is, Letitia forgets that her four-year-old sister, Charonna, is an undisputed angel, whereas Harry was just *born* scheming.

"Yep. That young," Hannah confirmed bleakly.

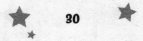

"I lost my favourite Polly Pocket doll. You know –
those small ones?"

"Sure." I shrugged, while Letitia nodded.

Of course I remembered. I still, ahem, had my
two Polly Pocket dolls in a box in the cupboard
back in my old bedroom. (It's not too cool to
admit that you can't quite bring yourself to throw
your old Polly Pockets out, when you're a
thirteen-year-old girl with a passion for indie and
classic rock music and a reputation for deep, dark
sarcasm.)

"Well, I found it – eventually," said Hannah, an
ominous glower darkening her face. "She was
wrapped up in one of Harry's nappies."

"Aw . . . Charonna used to do stuff like that!"
Letitia butted in brightly, blanking the fact that
this was the infamous Harry we were talking
about. "She loved putting her nappies on her dolls
and teddies and singing them lulla—"

"It was a *used* nappy!" Hannah butted back.

Yuck.

"Have you ever tried doing practical jokes back
to him, Hannah?" Letitia suggested.

Letty loves suggesting answers to problems,
mainly because she's addicted to problem pages
in magazines. Hannah, on the other hand, *hates*
being told what to do.

"Yeah, like *that'll* ever happen!" Hannah replied dismissively.

"You can't trick a trickster," I explained. "Harry always seems to be able to suss out when anyone's up to something. Isn't that right, Hannah?"

It's always like this when I get my two buddies together, which isn't very often. I like them, and they like me, but somehow they don't much like each *other*. So I end up being the go-between, explaining what the other meant, before one of them takes something the wrong way and slopes off in a huff. It's pretty tiring. But hey, I have to try to get them together once in a while, just in case there's some big breakthrough where they both realize the other one is actually OK.

And, whatever, I needed my room painted, and the more hands on deck, the better. . .

"Yeah, yeah – but I don't want to waste too many precious seconds of my life thinking about my wormy brother. Anyway . . . what's the latest on that Cormac guy, Sadie?" said Hannah, suddenly changing the subject, and giving me a wink.

The wink went unseen by Letitia, who had stopped painting long enough to wrestle open another bag of Kettle Chips.

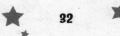

I knew what this was about. This was about Letitia having a giant crush on Cormac. As soon as we all saw him do his stand-up comedy routine on Highbury Fields, Letty had immediately sized him up as her new Fantasy Boyfriend (i.e. just one in a long LINE of Fantasy Boyfriends). Of course, Hannah had worked that out – since she was there too – but I'd made her *swear* she wouldn't tease Letty about it. Glad to see she'd remembered about the no-teasing promise. *Ha. . .*

"Latest what?" I said calmly, while widening my eyes at Hannah in a big "don't you dare!" glare.

Letty was now scrabbling on the floor, trying to gather up the crisps that had exploded from the bag when she'd pulled too hard at the mention of Cormac's name.

"Is he going to do another stand-up thing again?" said Hannah, pretending she didn't see my eyebrows levitating in a warning fashion. "Just wondering if he'll do the same routine, since it got a lot of laughs last time."

Ooh, now she was teasing me too.

Mainly 'cause the routine Cormac did last time was all *about* me.

Which was mortifying at the time – in front of

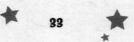

a whole bunch of curious, milling strangers in the park – but somehow not so bad after. It was kind of nice to be the focus of attention for once, instead of You-Know-Who (the You-Know-Who that I happened to be related to).

Speaking of You-Know-Who, I still wasn't so sure I liked the fact that his band was sort of named after me. *That* kind of exposure I could live without. . .

"He says he's been too busy to think about any comedy stuff," I told Hannah and, of course, Letty, who was silently hyperventilating as she (probably) imagined herself jet-setting round the world, as her husband – the world-famous comedian Cormac O'Connell – performed in equally world-famous venues in front of packed audiences. "There's been a big rush on dead people, apparently."

"Bleurgh. . ." groaned Hannah, jerked out of teasing mode by the grim reality of Cormac's day job. "Hey – I should tell Harry that I know an undertaker! He'd be *well* impressed. He's obsessed with stuff about death and anything gruesome at the moment. Have you ever seen that animated film *The Corpse Bride?* He's *nuts* about that. He's watched it about a mill—"

"BwuhuHUHUHIH! Hurrrr-ah-HURRR!"

It was an unearthly sound: like a cackling hyena morphed with a bellowing zombie.

"What's that?" asked Letitia, her face a picture of alarm, like the heroine in a horror movie. (Though heroines in horror movies tend to be in cheerleader outfits or something, not wearing Lisa Simpson nighties, shower caps on their heads, and cuddling a bag of sour cream and chive crisps for comfort.)

I knew *exactly* what it was. It was the horrible, blood-curdling, baying sound of Kennedy Jones *laughing*, the big baboon. Still, he was quite a *popular* big baboon; lots of the girls at their stage school apparently fancied Kennedy madly, which is why I guess he got a place in the dumb boy band alongside Sonny.

But it's bizarre; Kennedy has this weirdly wide face. How anyone can madly fancy someone who looks like a handsome frying pan is beyond me. Though apparently that's what lots of young Hollywood actors are like in the flesh: up-close, they're teeny-tiny with big lollipop heads.

I think I'll stick to lusting from afar over sulky members of rock bands. . .

"Don't worry – it's just Kennedy," I reassured Letty.

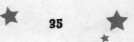

"BWAHHHHH, HURRRahHURRRRRRR!! HAAA-HAAAA!!"

Oh. That was quite a *lot* of bellowing. That wasn't just Kennedy and/or Sonny.

Uh-oh – I just remembered something: Mum had said earlier that Sonny was rehearsing again in the evening. I didn't realize that meant he'd be rehearsing *here*, at our house.

"I think it's all the lads who are in. . ."

I couldn't bring myself to say the name of the band.

"Sadie Rocks. . .?" chirped Letty helpfully, relaxing enough to nibble on a crisp now that she knew it was only boys and not werewolves in the hall outside.

"Yeah, them. Whatever they're called," I said, trying to sound casual.

Sadie Rocks. . . I sure wouldn't be the first in the queue to buy a band T-shirt with *that* on the front. I mean, my name, linked to a corny boy band – how was I going to stand the shame? If they ever got in the charts I'd have to change my name by deed poll.

"Ooh, d'you think any of them will be cute?" asked Hannah, her boy radar on sudden alert.

My upper lip slid into an automatic snarl. I didn't personally know the other three lads that

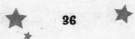

were in my brother's band, but I could guess they were pretty cute to look at. After all, that's the aim of boy bands, isn't it? As long as they're pretty, it doesn't matter if they can't play instruments, or if all there is between their ears is a windswept expanse of endless shallowness.

"What are they doing here?" asked Letty, pulling the door open a crack to catch a peek at them – but she was too late: I'd just heard the clunk of Sonny's door shutting.

"Rehearsing their songs," I said flatly.

"Yay! Let's go listen!!" suggested Hannah, dropping her paint roller back into its tray.

Actually, it could be quite entertaining, I decided. Earwigging on the band as they struggled to harmonize . . . that could be a fun decorating-break.

"Come on, then," I said, leading the way.

Five seconds later, we had our ears pressed against Sonny's bedroom door: Hannah and Letty standing either side, me hunkered down in a crouch, with Clyde my rabbit flopping up against me for a back scratch. (Clyde works like a stealth bomber: sensing movement anywhere in the house, then locking in and tracking down the source for a snuggle.)

Hmm. There seemed to be a lot of shuffling

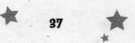

noises going on in Sonny's room, above the hubbub of bloke-chat.

"What d'you think they're doing now?" whispered Letty.

"Must be moving furniture," I whispered back. "Maybe they're making space to practise their dance routines?"

The very thought of five boys thumping about in Dad's old Bachelor Pad made me grin. (Even if I hadn't exactly grinned too much when Mum gave this room to Sonny, rather than me, for the very reason that he needed the space to practise. . . Practise being a show-off. Ho, ho, ho.)

"What're the other three boys like?" Hannah mouthed at me.

OK, so I knew a few facts 'cause of what I'd heard Sonny tell Mum and Will; i.e. the lads were called "Marcus", "Hal" and "Ziggy". The inverted commas are 'cause I *also* knew that their *real* names were Mark, Alan and Gordon. That was till Benny their teacher told them their own names weren't interesting enough for the band. Sonny already sounded "interesting", my brother had told Mum, acting all coy as if he wasn't chuffed about that or anything. And Kennedy? Well, he'd already changed his name from Kenneth *way* back when he first started at stage school. I think they must have advised him that girls might well fancy handsome frying pans, but not if they were called *Kenneth*.

"Well, apparently two of them have been on telly," I told my buddies in a hushed voice. "One of them was once on some hospital programme playing the part of a kid who got his head stuck in railings, and one of them was in an ad for medicine, playing a cold germ."

Letty and Hannah had both been staring at me transfixed at the mention of telly and associated fame, but as soon as I mentioned heads stuck in railings and cold germs, they started sniggering and didn't seem able to stop.

"Shhhh!" I giggled back, from my hunched-up position, "Stop it! They'll hear us!"

SWOOSH!

The speed with which the door was pulled open was nearly enough to make a girl and her paint roller topple over.

"What're you doing, Sadie?" Sonny demanded, standing almost star-shaped in the doorway, so that we couldn't get a proper peek into his room. Mind you, I didn't really want his mates to see *us*, now that I'd suddenly remembered we were dressed in too-small pyjamas.

But back to Sonny's question – what was I

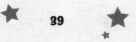

39

doing? I had to think quickly. I couldn't let him get the better of me.

"What does it *look* like we're doing?" I said casually, trying to buy time till something smarter tripped into my mind. Bluff, bluff, bluff. I held the paint roller over my chest so he couldn't see the "cute" teddy on my top.

"Spying on us?" suggested Sonny, resting his arms on the doorframe and staring down at me, crouched at his feet. Hannah and Letty were non-helpfully still giggling, and skipping backwards down the hall towards my new bedroom, with Clyde lolloping behind.

"Yeah, like you're *that* interesting, Sonny!" I said, straightening up, and opting for plain old sarcasm in place of a remotely decent excuse. "You know, you're *so* big-headed!!"

"Hey, why are you all wearing *pyjamas*?" my brother suddenly asked, annoyingly unfazed by what I'd just said to him.

"Oh . . . grow up, Sonny!" I snapped. "You're such a *loser*!"

That was lame – *uselessly* lame, in fact.

He'd got me, and he knew it.

And now Sonny was going in for the kill. . . He raised his eyebrows at me, and then the tiniest smirk started showing at the corner of his mouth.

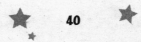

Uh-oh – I knew what was coming next. The one thing that always drove me *mad*!!

"MUM!!" he yelled casually. "SADIE SAID I WAS A—"

I didn't stay to hear the rest of his time-honoured telltale yell to our mother – mainly 'cause I could make out the rest of his band bursting into a cackle-a-thon in the background.

They'd all heard (from Sonny) about the run-ins me and him had. And he'd told them that the one way to wind me up was to yell the stupid "Sadie said. . ." phrase to Mum. That's when one of them (which one?) had come out with the sarky "sounds like Sadie rocks!" comment that gave them their stupid band name. Urgh. . .

OK, time for a tactical retreat.

"Right," I said firmly, slamming the door to my new room behind me.

"What are you going to do?" asked Letty, watching me as I swapped my roller for a paintbrush.

"*This*. . ."

I splodged a few half-a-metre high letters on the last unpainted wall.

"SONNY BIRD IS A BIG-NOSED NERK. . ."

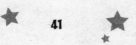

41

OK, it was *way* childish. But it made me feel a whole LOT better.

"Can you pass me my camera?" I asked Hannah, so I could save these soothing words long after the wall got painted over. . .

Small-time lies

Out of respect to Mum, I'd put on the most chilled, soothing, non-rock CD in my collection (The Beta Band Greatest Hits, if you wanted to know).

She wasn't really listening, though. She mostly filters out sounds that aren't classical music or Martha crying/cooing. Anyway, Mum was slightly distracted by what I was loading on my computer.

"You know, Sadie," she began, with a bundle of newly washed and ironed curtains in her arms, "I really wish you and Sonny would get on better."

I don't think she was particularly happy that I was using the "SONNY BIRD IS A BIG-NOSED NERK" photo as my screen-saver.

"We get on all right," I lied.

Mum is kind and dippy and a bit of a worrier, so I tend to play down how much Sonny bugs me, though I guess it's glaringly obvious sometimes.

"Hmm. Well, if you get on so well, why have

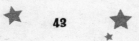

you written *that* about your brother?" As Mum spoke, she looked round at the soothing green walls and seemed to be trying to guess which one had had the offending brother-bashing words daubed on it. She wouldn't be able to tell, though. In fact, you could hardly believe this room was once bright blue and full of toast crumbs, dust balls and Arsenal Football Club and movie posters. After a Sunday morning's worth of hard labour by me and Mum and Will it was unrecognizable; even the smell was different – fresh paint from last night's "party" instead of the strange and inexplicable hamster-honk of boys. . .

"It's just a bit of fun," I lied again, clicking off the screen-saver to spare Mum's maternal feelings.

"Course it is!" said Will, as he lay flat out on the bed he'd dragged through earlier, and bounced Martha up and down on his tummy. "I mean, Sonny doesn't even *have* a big-nose!"

Will is nice. *Too* nice, sometimes. He's always trying to make everything sound super and great and "cool" (his favourite word), even if it's not – I think he thinks it's his duty as a stepdad. Or not-quite-stepdad, if you're going to get technical, since he and Mum haven't got round to getting married yet.

Actually, Mum and Dad haven't got round to getting *divorced* yet, if you want to get *hyper*-technical.

"Yeah, and 'nerk' is just a silly, funny word I made up," I joined in, trying to reassure Mum.

"No – 'nerk' is a real word," said Will. "It's slang from the 1950s or '60s, I think – but it's not used much any more. It means 'idiot'."

Mum bit her lip. She was probably doing a mental calculation of how many years it would be till me and/or Sonny left home, i.e. how many years of sibling stress she had to look forward to.

"Say cheese!!" I ordered her, picking up the camera at the side of my computer and pointing it at her.

She caved in to the enforced jollity and let one of her lovely smiles break out.

As soon as I snapped her, I moved the lens round to capture Martha in mid-air, hovering above Will and my stripy duvet cover.

And where was Clyde? I'd seen him hopping into my (new) room out of the corner of my eye when I was setting up the computer. . . Oh, there he was – SNAP! – chewing on the corner of one of my old Harry Potter books. I'd have to get those up on a bookshelf (though first I'd need a bookshelf).

"Right, let's get this room finished," Mum said suddenly, sounding more organized than she usually does. "I'll get the curtains up, and, Will – you get on with the shelves. Sadie, can you take Martha out of the way, so she doesn't try and climb stepladders and play with powertools?"

"Sure," I said, scooping my baby sister up into my arms. "Let's go out in the garden and try and get a nice photo of you with the flowers, hmmm?"

Martha tugged hard on my hair as an answer (I took that as a yes), and we headed off, hardly sparing a glance at Sonny's closed bedroom door (poor lamb – he was still sleeping, exhausted from a hard day's bad harmonizing yesterday, I guess).

SNAP! Poor Dog – stuck in her cage in the living room with her lampshade collar on wasn't her best look. But I had a corkboard leaning against my bedroom wall which needed filling with all-new photos for my all-new room, of all my favourite people – as well as furry *non-*people.

Moving on out to the garden, with Martha perched happily on my hip, I gazed around for photographic inspiration. But there just seemed to be a lot of laundry on the line and a bunch of dull, leafy bushes that were in between flowering.

"*I* know," I said to Martha, heading towards the bottom of the garden and the old iron railings there. "Let's go to a magical, faraway land!"

Carefully, to avoid baby-head-bumpage, I wriggled through the bent and broken railing and came out in the little copse that separated our back garden from the magical, faraway land beyond. OK, so it was just the bog-standard graveyard, but Martha was only seven months old, so I could safely lie to her as much as I wanted.

"Did you know," I whispered to her, pointing to the low-hanging branches of my pet Christmas tree, "that tiny, fairy-sized hippos live up there?"

"Urgle!" muttered Martha, settled quite snugly on my hip and playing with the button on her cardie.

SNAP! With my one free hand, I pointed the camera directly up, capturing a hippo-free view of greenery, with glimpses of blue sky and fluffy cloud beyond. Another one for my corkboard gallery.

"Hey, I bet you didn't know that all those chunky headstones there are made of fudge!" I fibbed some more, as I carried Martha out of the copse and into the graveyard itself.

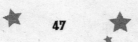

47

"Wooooh-uh!" Martha cooed, her eyes vaguely following the finger that I was pointing.

(I promise I'll ditch the small-time lies when she's big enough to understand what I'm saying.)

"And see all those flowers? They're made of candy! Do you want to go nibble the pretty candy flowers?"

Martha gurgled happily and gummed my shoulder hard. Ouch.

Rose bushes, fuchsia bushes, dandelions, daisies and vases of cut flowers left by relatives . . . there was plenty of petal action going on out here. (Even if I'd been fibbing about the nibbling possibilities of them.)

"Let's get a pretty photo of you in the magical, faraway land, then," I said to my baby sister, casting my eyes around for a good setting.

Suddenly keen to explore, Martha wriggled and squiggled in my arms.

"Here – I like this!" I said, lowering her down so that her back was resting up against a peachy-granite headstone with tumbling orange nasturtiums all around its base.

Martha smiled and cooed as I shook some tangles of nasturtium loose and draped them across her lap.

"Lovely!" I grinned down at her. "I'm sure. . ."

I glanced up at the writing on headstone: "*In memory of my dearly beloved brother Edward. . .*"

"I'm sure dearly beloved Edward won't mind us taking a few photos here, since he's been dead for. . ."

A quick check again, this time of the date, followed by some lightning-fast, brain-draining mental arithmetic.

". . .ooh, a hundred and six years."

SNAP! SNAP! SNAP!

As I clicked the cuteness of my fat-cheeked little sis, I thought how funny it would be for me to refer to Sonny as "my dearly beloved brother". No chance. "My dearly beloved *nerk*", maybe.

(I really liked nerk; I was determined to use it lots and get it right back in fashion).

And then I stopped laughing to myself and crouched down beside Martha. I felt bad – after all, the nerk was her brother too.

"Y'know, I *do* get on with Sonny *sometimes*," I told her, even though I knew the only words she really understood were "food" (always got big smiles) and "let's change that nappy!" (cue tears and wailing). "I mean, growing up, I always liked it when. . ."

I struggled to think.

When he fell asleep in the back of the car on

long journeys, and I got Mum and Dad to myself for once? Happy days. . .

"Seriously, I liked it when we were little and we used to put on these silly shows for Mum and Dad and Gran."

Yeah, I liked that a lot – till Sonny started ordering me around, and tried to get me to practise, practise, practise the dance routines and speeches he'd made up till I was perfect, which I was never going to be. (Even way back then, you didn't need a crystal ball to figure out that I'd be the dull, ordinary twin and Sonny would be the one about to sign a record deal at the age of thirteen. . .)

"Still, when it comes to music, we get along, I suppose," I carried on, looking up again at the nice words carved in memory of Edward. "As long as he's not nicking any of my CDs, of course. . ."

Martha did this hiccup-y giggle, like she does when a plastic pot of her favourite baby gloop comes out of the microwave, or if anyone mentioned the "f" word ("*food*", I meant!) in general.

Uh-oh.

Seemed like Martha had decided it was snack-time. I glanced down to see her stuffing handfuls of non-candy-flavoured flowers in her mouth, orange petals sticking to her cheeks and chin.

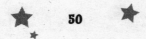

It would have made a great photo for my corkboard – if I wasn't so busy rushing her from the magic, faraway land back to the house.

Anyone know how poisonous nasturtiums are, exactly. . .?

You are now entering a mad phase. . .

"Urgh, you're not actually *drooling*, are you, Hannah?"

Hannah put her tongue back in her mouth and took her hands off the glass window.

"I'm *acting*, dahling – can't you tell?!" she replied, all pretend posh and indignant, tucking her perma-straightened long dark hair behind her ears.

"OK – do it again, then!"

I lifted my camera up, and Hannah struck her pose, limpeted with lust against the window of her favourite clothes shop in Islington's shop-a-delic Upper Street. We were getting a *lot* of strange looks from Monday afternoon shoppers in our North London part of the world.

SNAP!

"Got it!" I said, checking out the image on the viewfinder. There – another shot I'd get round to printing out and sticking on my corkboard

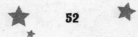

sometime soon. Almost without realizing it, it seemed like I'd found a pretty cool new hobby.

"And what if I go like *this*?" Hannah struck another pose, mimicking the mannequin in the window of the shop but adding her own unique edge (i.e. sucking her cheeks in and crossing her eyes).

"Great!" I said, snapping again. Hannah's as pretty as Letitia (and vice versa), but about a million times less self-conscious. When we'd met up after school today, she'd thrown herself into my mini-photo project like she was Kate Moss's funnier sister. (When I'd pointed the camera at Letitia at lunchtime, all I'd got was a shot of her giggling behind her hand. And then giggling behind her upturned lunch tray, when she saw I wasn't going to stop.)

"And how about thi – *ohhhhh*. . .!"

Weird – Hannah seemed about to throw herself recklessly into another who-cares-if-people-are-staring? pose and then sort of, well, deflated. I lowered the camera, and noticed that she was half-heartedly waving at someone behind me. Swivelling around, all I could make out was slow-moving traffic and strolling shoppers.

Ah. . . the slow-moving traffic. It was slow because a sleek black hearse was gliding its way

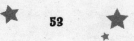

53

along Upper Street. It looked elegant, impressive and depressing all at once, a bit like a gloomy shark.

The only touches of colour were wreaths of cream and yellow roses leaning against the coffin in the back – and a flash of luminous orange hair above a black suit in the front.

Like Hannah, I found myself waving a limp hand, as if I was flapping a dead fish around in the air. I guess waving cheerfully back wasn't an option for Cormac. Instead, he gave us both the tiniest of nods hello – then the gloomy shark-mobile purred by.

"What a *bizarre* job," mumbled Hannah.

What a relief my little sister hadn't ended up in one of those, I thought to myself with a lurch, as the hearse moved smoothly away, and I remembered yesterday's poisoning panic.

Martha hadn't died, as you might have guessed by now. She hadn't even needed her tiny stomach pumped, though she'd been gagging badly by the time I'd hurtled into the house with her, yelling my head off for Mum and Will.

Though the first person to potentially give First Aid was Gran, who was in the kitchen, freshly arrived for a visit and getting the kettle on (her default setting).

"WENEEDTOGOTOTHEHOSPITAL!MART

HA'SEATENLOADSOFTHESE!!" I'd babbled at high speed, holding up Martha and a handful of semi-chewed flowers as evidence.

"Ah, now, calm yourself," Gran had said in her laid-back Irish lilt, taking Martha from me. "Babies just don't like the pepper-y taste!"

"The pepper-y taste of *POISON*?!" I'd yelped.

I hate losing my cool. I really do. Specially when it turned out that nasturtiums are not just non-poisonous, but "can actually be used in salads" according to Gran (yeah, if you're *mad*). And specially when your nerk of a brother comes in at the end of the conversation, i.e. the bit where you still look panicked, yet slightly idiotic. And as anyone with half a brain knows, panicked and idiotic is *so* not a good look. . .

SNAP! Lost in thought, I took a photo of the retreating hearse, and only realized a second after how bad taste that was. I'd have to delete it, along with the shot from this lunchtime of the yellow plastic lunch tray with Letty's dark cornrows just visible over the top.

"Do you think Cormac likes horror movies?" Hannah interrupted my whirring brain.

"Why? Are you planning to ask him out to one?" I asked her. "Don't tell me *you* have a crush on him too!"

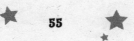

I knew she didn't. It was just fun to tease her and watch her squirm.

"No!" Hannah squirmed (there – see?). "I mean, I bet he's got a thing about movies with death scenes. Don't you think? I bet him and his brother sit and watch horror movies every night, since about a zillion people get killed in every one of 'em!"

Hey, it was a fun idea, and the whole way back to my house, me and Hannah came up with as many movies with death scenes in as we could think of – even though I knew for sure that Cormac was more into comedy DVDs. But what was entertainingly gruesome about that?

"*I* know: *Titanic*! Lots of people died in that. And, like, really *tragically*," said Hannah happily, as we bumbled into my house, ready to investigate whatever Will had come up with for tea.

"OK – you win." I shrugged. During the stomp back to mine, we'd covered death scores in gory movies (i.e. zombies and non-zombies in *Shaun of the Dead*), fantasy movies (i.e. endless massed armies in the *Lord of the Rings* trilogy, and tearjerking movies (i.e. *Stepmom* – Letitia was in absolute *floods* the one time we watched that).

But my last effort – Captain Hook becoming a

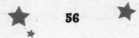

crocodile's lunch in *Peter Pan* – couldn't beat Hannah's. Tragic loss-of-life based on a true story always beats stupid-and-dumb hands down.

"Hi!" I called out, hearing a chatter of voices in the living room.

"Hi, Sadie! Come on through!" Mum's voice called back. "We've got a visitor!"

A visitor, eh?

Mum never referred to friends – hers, Will's, mine or Sonny's – as visitors, so that ruled them out. And it sure didn't mean Gran, who Mum and Will considered part of the family and who was free to come and go and she pleased (pretty funny, really, since she wasn't related to either Mum or Will, being *Dad's* mum).

No, "we've got a visitor" was a code to me and/or Sonny. It meant "whatever you do, don't come in the room picking your nose/ swearing/only wearing your pants".

I couldn't wait to see who it was, and who I had to behave for.

"Hi, honey! Hi, Hannah!" Mum said hyper-brightly.

Bizarre. It was as if aliens had infiltrated the room and conducted some freaky experiment on everyone in it. 'Cause they (Mum, Will, Martha, Gran and Sonny, plus that cheesily handsome

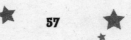

bloke sitting on the armchair nearest the window) were *all* grinning the same *huge* matching grin. It looked unnervingly strange.

"This is Benny!" Mum chirped, wafting a hand towards Mr Cheesy Handsome.

Ah, Benny. Sonny's new tutor at stage school, and the man with the plan for the junior boy band. There was a reality show on TV a while back, where people were singing and acting their hearts out to win a place in a West End musical. I really enjoyed watching it (for all the wrong reasons); everyone on it was super-corny and oozed that oily "I'm quite attractive and *boy* do I know it!" charm. Benny, with his soft curly brown hair, dimples and shiny-toothed smile was exactly like one of those West End musical wannabes.

No wonder Sonny looked up to him so much.

"Hey, Sadie! Guess what?" Sonny beamed at me. " 'Cause you're never going to be able to guess. 'Cause this is just dead cool and everything. Go on – just try and guess!"

Urgh, I was being dazzled by too much brightness. I could do with having a pair of sunglasses on.

"I don't want to guess," I answered flatly, even though I was slightly intrigued about what was

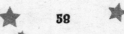

going on, and what Mr Cheesy Handsome was doing sitting in our living room, making himself comfortable with a cup of tea and a slab of Gran's home-made lemon cake.

"Benny's just told us we're definitely signing our record deal a week today!" Sonny blurted, full of the joys of being potentially famous.

"Ooh!" said Hannah behind me, clapping her hands together, and automatically joining in with the manic grinning.

"But you already *knew* that was going to happen soon," I said, proud of my non-participating smile.

"Yeah, but there's more—"

"By the way, how much are they going to pay you?" I interrupted, probably sounding like one of the agents that worked in the booking office at the stage school.

I noticed the freaky alien grins start fading at that comment, like my words were an icy wind, blasting away the happy glitter of fame. But hey, Mum always says I'm the dependable one, the sensible twin, so wasn't it my job to ask the unglamorous but important questions?

"I've run the contract by the theatre school directors, and they seem fine with the offer," said Benny, stepping up to (sort of) answer me. "And,

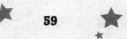

of course, all the parents of the boys involved have a chance to look over the contracts and approve them before they're signed."

OK, so *that's* what that pile of papers was on the coffee table. Whoops! Better not get any coffee or lemon cake-sticky fingers on that!

"And *because* all the parents have to do the signing on behalf of the boys," Mum continued, "the record company want to invite everyone's families into their offices next Monday—"

"—with a party afterwards!" added Sonny.

Good grief, he looked like he was just about ready to *explode*. I mean, I *was* pleased for my brother (in my own hard-to-spot way), but I couldn't help being cynical. I bet the record company wasn't going to pay the boys all *that* much. I mean, Dad had told me plenty of rock 'n' roll tales over the years, some of them about hugely famous bands who'd earned spectacularly little, thanks to greedy record companies.

So the lot that were signing Sonny's band; did they think they could throw some cheesy party for all the mums and dads and sisters and brothers with a few crisps thrown in, and everyone would be so chuffed and star-struck that they wouldn't notice that all the boys have been contracted for forty years and were being paid twenty-five pence a week or something?

"And Sonny's going on this really cool bonding course with Benny and the other lads this weekend!" said Will, bouncing, bouncing, bouncing Martha on his knees. (Hope she hadn't had too much of that lemon cake or she might barf all over those very same knees, and ruin the sugary atmosphere.)

"Yeah! It's like this . . . this . . . what is it like again?" Sonny started and then stopped, glancing at Benny for help.

"We're going to this centre in Hertfordshire, where they do these amazing group bonding sessions, based on Native American rituals for young warriors."

Good grief. That was the single most naff, cheesy thing I'd ever heard.

It sounded like the punchline of a comedy routine that Cormac could do.

It was on the tip of my tongue to say, "You're kidding me, right?", till I saw all those shiny happy faces still beaming away.

"Another piece of lemon cake, Benny?" Gran offered helpfully. "Are you going to sit down, girls?"

"Um, we've got homework to do. C'mon,

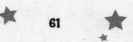

Hannah," I said, grabbing my friend and retreating out of the Room of Grins, before anyone could rouse themselves enough to point out that Hannah and I weren't even at the same *school*, never mind in the same class, so we'd hardly have the same homework to do together.

Still, me and Hannah *did* get busy, with a project that you could say was educational. It certainly took a bit of research. . .

"SADIE!!!"

That was Sonny's voice, half an hour later, when Benny had gone and Hannah and I were just about to get stuck into Will's veggie lasagne. Sonny had nipped to the loo, which happened to be right by his bedroom. He'd seen his door then.

"SADIE!!" he shouted again, from the first floor landing. "DID YOU PUT *CHEESE* ON MY DOOR?!"

"*Cheese?*" Mum frowned across the table at me. She obviously imagined I'd squished a handful of Dairylea all over the place.

"It's *photos* of cheese, Mum," I explained, as if printing out and taping pictures of cheese on to your brother's bedroom door was the most natural thing in the world.

I could see the word "why?" about to pop out of Mum's mouth, but Hannah got in there first.

"We went online and found thirty-two different types of cheese," she said conversationally. "And there were *heaps* more we could've done, but we ran out of space to stick them up. Isn't that amazing that there's so many types of cheese?"

"Cheesily *handsome* cheese, too!" I muttered out of the side of my mouth.

"Thirty-two? That's cool!" said Will, with an encouraging nod of his head.

"It's just a joke, Mum," I said with a shrug. "IT'S JUST A JOKE, SONNY!"

And with that yell, I nonchalantly carried on with my lasagne.

Mum looked at me strangely, like she was reappraising her eldest daughter – as if she was thinking that I was less sensible and dependable than I used to be, and perhaps entering a slightly *mad* phase.

And, actually, I quite liked that. . .

A huge case of *non*-like

Eleanor Cooper did a lot of hair-swishing. She oozed confidence. You got the feeling that at the age of sixteen, she'd been a proper Miss Unfeasibly Popular, with a fan club of lads gazing longingly at her from afar.

She still had an air of that, though she seemed to be oblivious to the fact that she was now fifty-ish, and the boys at school called her Gandalf.

Miss Cooper was also the teacher in our year that you had to get permission slips from, when you needed to get time off for dentist and doctor appointments, or holidays in term time or whatever.

She was pretty strict. Well, I guess she had to be; Mr Green, who did all that stuff before her, once let Jack Higgins off school loads in one year and didn't seem to notice that Jack's gran had apparently died three times. (Poor her.)

So I was pretty sure that Miss Cooper was going to take one look at the letter from my mum, asking for time off next Monday afternoon to go to Sonny's contract signing, and tear the thing up in front of my eyes and set fire to it. Probably.

You'd think Mum would know better, being a Head of Department herself (music), but then again, when it comes to anything to do with Sonny, she turns into an adoring, fluffy-headed "that's-my-boy!" stage mom.

(By the way, how was Mum going to get time off at *her* school? Did teachers need permission slips? Or maybe she could just write *herself* one. . .)

I hovered with my knuckles half a centimetre from Mrs Cooper's door and tried to work up the courage to knock. Sadly, the courage stayed wherever it was and refused to show itself.

Dropping my head, I took a deep breath . . . and my eyes settled on one severely scrawled-on beige-ish, dirty-ish canvas school bag. *Mine*, of course. Well, *Dad's*, technically. It was thirty-something years old, and had Dad's favourite bands' names written all over it (he said it was just what any self-respecting teenage music fan did during dull lessons in the 1970s).

And the scrawls were thusly:

Talking Heads
The Clash
Blondie
Ian Dury and the Blockheads
The Pretenders
David Bowie
Siouxsie Sioux and the Banshees
The Jam

I'd added a handful more in the few spaces that were left:

Arctic Monkeys
Foo Fighters
Gorillaz
Kasabian

Pah.

You know, I couldn't do it. I couldn't stand the thought of Miss Cooper turning down my permission for absence for such a piffly, frivolous reason. And in the unlikely event that I did get permission, I was one hundred per cent paranoid that word might get out, and everyone in my class, my year, my *school* would know that my brother was going to be in a corny boy band. And a junior boy band at that, i.e. the kind that's really aimed at little kids and grannies. I just couldn't face it – especially since I knew the one, half-decent reputation I had was for knowing my stuff when it came to music.

I mean, yeah, so everyone at school would know eventually – *if* Sonny's band made it, that is – but I'd worry about it *then*.

"Can I help you, Sadie?"

Miss Cooper had swished her door open alarmingly quickly, without a pad of a footstep or a squeak of a floorboard as warning. It was almost as if she'd hovered her way magically to the door, just like the real Gandalf might have done.

"I just. . ."

Help, help, help.

Think, think, think.

Lie, lie, lie.

". . .dropped a pound coin somewhere here, but I can't find it," I said, scrunching up the letter from Mum in the safety of my pocket. "But it must have rolled away."

"Oh, dear." (Hair flick.) "Good luck with that, then, Sadie!"

And with another flick, Miss Cooper strode off,

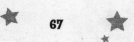

with some important file or other tucked under her arm.

"What was Gandalf saying to you?" asked Letitia, ambling along the corridor from the direction of the loos. (Whenever she gets her cornrows redone, she obsesses about her roots growing in all curly and ruining the sleek look. No mirror goes ungazed in, in the pursuit of rogue root regrowth.)

"I was supposed to give her this," I explained, handing Letty the crumpled piece of paper. "But I bottled out and gave her some old waffle about dropping money and looking for it."

"Oh, how much did you drop?" said Letty, looking around on the floor for a stray, shiny coin while unravelling Mum's letter.

"Are you kidding me?" I asked her, rolling my eyes.

Letty can be *such* a ditz sometimes; it really cracks me up.

But she's not so bad; she giggled at her own numptyness, then started to read – until her attention was caught by something else.

"Sadie, your bag just wobbled!"

In other words, my phone was set to vibrate.

"It's only Hannah," I said, reading the text message on the screen, and trying to sound uninterested in my other friend, in case my *current* friend got the hump. (I tell you, it's pretty tricky having friends who aren't, well, *friends*.)

"Yeah? So what does *she* want, then?"

Ha. Letitia was aiming to sound casual and only marginally curious, but the fact that she emphasized the word "she" in that sentence gave her – and her dislike of Hannah – away.

Though maybe "dislike" was too strong a word. Maybe it was more of a big case of *non*-like. It wasn't as if Letty and Hannah ever argued or bitched about each other (they wouldn't do that in front of me), but they always acted in this slightly frosty, mildly competitive way in each other's company, like two strangers made to sit side-by-side before being interviewed for the same job.

"Oh, no. . ." My heart sank like a stone weighted down by rocks when I scrolled down Hannah's message. "Her dad's away on business, and her mum's had to change shifts at the hospital. Hannah's got to babysit her brother, Harry, for a couple of hours after school today and tomorrow."

"Ah, that's *bad*."

Yeah, and what Letty had just said was a *vast* understatement.

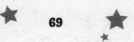

"It gets worse," I mumbled, reading on. "She can't face doing it on her own. She wants *me* to come now and help her."

There was a moment's silence as Letty and I both remembered the hideousness of the cling-film-over-the-toilet-seat moment. Let's just say there was wee, there was slipping, there was total and utter embarrassment, followed by a vow never to set foot in Hannah's house again.

"You're going to do it, though, right?" asked Letty.

"Duh! I'd rather eat my sister's nappies!" I groaned.

Letty looked me in the eye. She has these huge melted-chocolate eyes that are guaranteed to make you feel instantly guilty, even if you've nothing to feel guilty about. Disney or Pixar should think about using her as a template for their next adorably cute character. A baby racoon or something.

"But she's your friend! You've got to help your friends when they're in trouble!" said my very own guilt-tripping racoon. "And I bet you've moaned to her *loads* about Sonny!

See, this is why I like Letitia so much, even when she's saying stuff I don't really want to hear. She's just a much *nicer* person than me. I

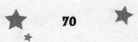

mean, she didn't even *like* Hannah – or at least only *non*-liked her – and yet she was still able to empathize with her over the serious trouble she was in. And Hannah *was* in trouble. Being left alone with Harry, *anything* could happen. She might find slugs in her shoes. Her Diet Coke might taste of washing-up liquid. There might be a Tupperware box full of green gloop balanced precariously on the top of the bathroom door.

Of course, all of that could *still* happen with me there, but at least she'd have sympathetic company, as she removed the slugs, spat out the fizzy drink and wiped green gloop from her face.

"You're right," I mumbled, texting back at the same time. I *had* to try harder to be as kind and thoughtful as Letty.

Less sarcasm, and more kindness, I thought to myself, as I zapped off the message offering my babysitting support services to Hannah.

"Ooh, how exciting! I didn't realize your brother's band were going to be signing their record contract next *week*!" cooed Letty, her Disney eyes scanning the crumpled letter. "How brilliant is *that*?"

"As brilliant as having a nail hammered directly

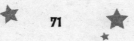

into your skull," I grumbled, snatching the letter back and crumping it into a tight ball.

Oh, well. I'd just have to practise this nice, kind, non-sarcastic thing *another* time. . .

Beware of the bear traps

Deep breath in, deep breath out.

Deep breath in, deep breath out.

He's a ten-year-old boy – don't let him get to you. Don't take any notice if he tries to tease you about the cling-film incident. Don't take any notice of him, period. You are here for your best mate and that's all that matters. . .

As I waited outside Hannah's front door – the ding-dong of the doorbell ominously fading away – I wasn't *completely* convinced that my pep-talk to myself would do any good.

"Sadie! Hi! Come in!"

Hannah answered the door with the nervous, glassy-eyed look of a character from a horror movie. She was like some hapless teenage girl who has an axe murderer hidden in the house, but is sworn to secrecy (by the axe murderer) on pain of death.

I came in – warily. It wasn't that I truly

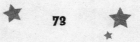

believed there was an axe murderer on the loose at Number 50, oh no. I was on the lookout for far more credible dangers, like bear traps or grand pianos suspended on flimsy ropes or burning hot oil being sprayed out of water pistols.

Well, Harry was getting older, so who knew when his kid-like dumb gags might mutate into something more extreme?

"How're you doing?" I asked Hannah, meaning, of course, "Has Harry done anything to you yet? Are you still in one piece?"

Hannah knew. She understood without me having to spell it out.

"So far, so . . . nothing. Can't quite believe it!" she whispered back. Aha – if she was whispering, it could mean Harry was within listening distance.

"Where is he?" I asked, in a cautious undertone.

"He's in there. . ." said Hannah, pointing to the living room.

Aha. A slight gap. I peeked in and saw Harry sitting about five centimetres from the TV screen, engrossed in some movie that sounded loud, with a grinning character who seemed to be oozing *slime* from his face.

"He found this old video at the back of the cupboard," Hannah explained under her breath. "It's called *Beetlejuice*. He's obsessed with it."

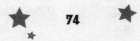

74

With that, she backed off, and motioned me to follow her upstairs.

As I padded up the stripy patterned stair carpet behind her I wracked my brains, pretty sure I'd seen a bit of *Beetlejuice* once on Film Four or some movie channel or something.

"It's a comedy about dead people, so Harry thinks it's great, of course," said Hannah, turning and talking to me over her shoulder.

"Yeah . . . I remember it now," I told her. "The time I saw it, I got freaked out by some space worm/monster things that surround the main characters' house."

"Well, Harry's just mad on the main guy in it, 'cause he's not just dead, but he's dead *mean* too."

Mmm . . . what a perfect hero for Harry, I thought, as we arrived on the first-floor landing.

Hannah's bedroom was on the left, with a soft, cream-coloured fabric flower stuck on it with her name spelt out in sparkly gold thread.

Harry's room was directly opposite. On *his* door was a felt-pen drawing of the Grim Reaper, leaning on a hockey stick. Oops – no, I guess it was meant to be a scythe. . .

"But the whole death thing is getting a bit nuts," said Hannah, surprising me by putting her hand on the door-handle to her brother's room instead of hers. "I mean, you've got to see *this*!"

With a quick safety-check glance back down the stairs, Hannah pushed open the softly creaking door to Harry's room.

Oooh.

Even with the Scooby Doo wallpaper, bats would've been quite at home here.

"I knew he'd got into morbid stuff – I mean, he's asked me a zillion questions about Cormac since I mentioned him. But check it out . . . last time I went in here it was all Power Rangers and Transformers posters on his walls!"

Not any more. We both wandered in and stared around us. There was a movie poster for *The Corpse Bride* (an animation Hannah said her brother was mad on), a couple more of a zombie movie I'd never heard of, and a Dr Who poster featuring a creature that definitely looked on the wrong side of alive. As well as those, there were lots of Harry's own artworks of ghosts, headstones, coffins and Frankenstein-type monsters.

Basically, it looked like the sort of room that Hannah and me had joked about as being the perfect morbid setting for *Cormac* and his funeral director brother to live in.

"Isn't it freaky?" Hannah whispered, walking

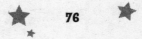

around, and letting her fingertips glide over a fluttery paper model skeleton. "What do you think is going on in Harry's head?"

Part of me wanted to say that a fascination with death was pretty normal growing-up stuff, specially for boys (like the stage when they're about five, and it's all bums *this* and willies *that*). But glancing around . . . it *was* all a little creepy.

"Well, I think it means he's either going to grow up as a Goth, an undertaker or a serial killer," I advised my friend.

Hannah grinned.

"You're going to *love* this," she continued. "He was asking Mum about embalming fluid this morning over breakfast. He was saying that he might try and see if they've got a book on how you use it in the school library!"

"What, does he think he'll find *Embalming for the Under-Tens*' filed after *Double Act* and right before *Fantastic Mr Fox*?" I sniggered softly, before turning and escaping from the mausoleum. I needed daylight. I needed a drink (preferably soap-free).

And that's when I tripped right over the piece of string that Harry had stealthily stretched across his bedroom doorway while me and Hannah had chatted, right at ankle level.

Grrr. So it wasn't a bear trap or a grand piano suspended by a flimsy rope or boiling oil being sprayed out of a water pistol, but it wasn't much fun either.

"Harry!! Wait till I tell Mum!" Hannah shouted, as she helped me up.

As I rubbed my carpet-grazed chin, I watched Harry hurtle down the stairs, and tried to estimate his height.

Yep, a metre-high coffin would do. Maybe me and Hannah could club together and get a discount on one from McConnell & Sons, seeing as we knew one of the sons.

It would be a lovely addition to Harry's room. We could get him to lie in it for fun. Then get the lid on quick and screw him in there for good. . .

Harry who?

"It's like a branch of an electrical store styled by a granny!" said Hannah, gazing around Dad's living room.

She was right. Dad's state-of-the-art telly was nearly as big as a Smart car, plus he had all those stacks of turntables and CD players with a stupidly large amount of speakers to go with them. (Don't you only need *two* speakers?)

"What's that smell?"

I ignored Harry *and* his question. The answer – if I'd wanted to give it to him – was one of those plug-in air fresheners with a scent like sherbet-y chemicals, the sort that are so sickly sweet they end up giving you a thumping headache after an hour. An addition by Dad's flatmate (Gran), of course.

But I'd decided the only way I could deal with horrible Harry was to pretend he didn't exist. I mean, in the past I'd tried to put Hannah's little

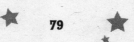

brother in his place by blasting him with laser beams of sarcasm, but he'd used a force field of stupidity and "got-you!" grins to repel them. So from now on, I was going to treat the little nerk as if he were invisible.

"What's this?"

Nope. Not a chance, Harry. The friction burn on my chin might prove his existence, but in every other way, he was a non-person to me.

"Yeah, what's this door doing here, Sadie?" asked Hannah, practically squashing her nose against the metal-framed glass door, alongside her brother. Outside of it (and the large window with a view of shop backyards) was an open metal staircase.

"It's a fire escape," I explained, figuring it was OK to answer if the question came from my friend. "If you go *down*, it comes out at the undertaker's, and if you go *up*, it takes you to Cormac's flat."

"Ooh, really?" Hannah turned her head around, with a swish of her long dark hair. Her eyes were suspiciously sparkly, and I half-expected her to suggest we inch up the steps SAS-style and spy into the flat above.

"Fancy getting the telephoto lens and snapping some top-secret shots?" I joked, raising my eyes to

the ceiling, and then down at the camera I'd just plonked on the glass and chrome side table (next to the "lovely" ornament of a lady in a pastel crinoline).

Hannah looked for a second like she might be considering it. Then, "Nah!", she said with a grin, as reality kicked in and she realized how dodgy that could be. I mean, imagine if the first sighting of Cormac's funeral director brother was of him in his boxers, as he changed out of his black work suit!

"What's this for?"

"Don't know. Don't touch it," Hannah ordered Harry, slapping his hand away from the temptingly shiny buttons on Dad's amp.

"Can I have a sandwich?"

"Come and see the rest of the place," I said to Hannah, motioning her to follow me, while I blanked Harry.

The guided tour this Wednesday afternoon was happening a) 'cause even though he'd lived here for nearly a month now, this was the first time Hannah had seen Dad's new flat, and b) we'd decided that it was possibly safer to babysit Harry *outside* of his house. Remove him from his playground of practical jokes, and he wouldn't be so obnoxious. We hoped.

"Are we having tea here?" Harry's voice trailed from the living room, as me and Hannah stepped into the room at the front of the building, with its three arched windows and a view of red London buses trundling along on the busy road outside.

"Dad's bedroom," I said, throwing my arm out wide to show off the large, sprawling, teenage boy's bedroom that belonged to my forty-seven-year-old father.

He'd be home from work any minute (I'd let myself in with one of the two sets of spare keys he'd had made for me and Sonny). I'd taken my camera so I could get a photo of him for the corkboard in my room back at home. Maybe I'd get him to lean up against that black Pink Floyd poster with the sort of rainbow triangle. It would clash nicely, if he was wearing one of his favourite vintage Hawaiian shirts. And hey, I could move the lava lamp into shot at the same time, for maximum colour overkill.

"Wow, I'd love a room this big!" said Hannah, waving at an old lady in the top deck of a passing No. 19 bus.

Next, the bathroom.

"It's very . . . *fluffy*," said Hannah, eyeing up the mega-tufted peach bath and toilet mats.

"I might have known. Gran'll probably be

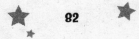

buying a set of yellow rubber duckies for Dad next . . ." I muttered.

And, then of course, the spare room, where Gran had made herself at home.

"Isn't this just a sort of cupboard?" asked Hannah, glancing around the smallest box room known to man, into which Gran had magically managed to squash a bed, a chest of drawers and some random bric-a-brac.

"Well, if she ever ends up in jail, she'll be quite at home in a cell after this!"

Ha – the thought of my gran ever doing anything bad enough to land her in jail was pretty funny. Since she retired as a school dinner lady last year, she'd thrown herself into helping out in a charity shop a few days a week, cake-making for any friends and neighbours within a ten-kilometre radius, and doting on my sister, Martha. Oh, and taking care of her ickle son now, of course.

Actually, perhaps unnecessary mollycoddling of a grown man is a criminal offence? "M'lud, I put it to you that the defendant, one Mrs Joan Bird, is guilty of cutting her adult son's toast into eggy soldiers and testing the temperature of his bath water with her elbow."

Maybe she was looking at a lengthy stretch in

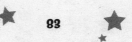

nearby Holloway prison after all. Maybe I'd have to smuggle in a file baked in a lemon cake of her own recipe. . .

"What about the kitchen?" asked Hannah, backing into the hall.

"Kitchen*ette*. Blink and you'll miss it. It's back through the living room," I told her.

Ah, the living room. Which was looking a little *emptier* than when we'd left it.

"Harry?!" yelled Hannah, spotting the open fire escape door. "*HARRY!!!*"

We both bolted over, clattering out on to the metal landing. Hannah glanced up, I glanced down.

"What're are you *doing*?" I hissed in a panic. I couldn't pretend Harry was pleasantly invisible now, not since he was currently attempting something that was quite possibly *criminal*.

"Aww . . . I can't see anything! They've got the blinds shut!!" Harry groaned, lowering MY camera from his face.

The staircase juddered metallically as two stressed thirteen-year-olds thundered down it to grab a thrill-seeking, ghoulish ten-year-old and bundle him back up the stairs sharpish.

"What d'you think you're playing at?" Hannah hissed at him, yanking him towards Dad's flat with an iron grip on his arm. I was behind, one hand in the small of his back, the other holding the camera I'd just reclaimed.

"I just wanted to try and get a photo of a dead bo—"

"Hello?"

The hello was coming from the open window in the flat above Dad's. Cormac's hand was visible, pushing the handle of a window pane open. And now there was the rattle of a key in a lock; he would be out on the stairwell any second.

"We're going – I'm taking him home!" Hannah whispered urgently, shoving her brother into Dad's living room, where I saw her grab up jackets and school bags in one panicked swoop. I didn't have time for byes. Straightaway, I had to launch into hellos.

"Hi! Only me!" I said cheerfully, which was uncomfortable for me since cheerful always feels a bit fake.

What can I say I've been doing? I fretted silently at high speed.

Why would I have been clunking about here on the stairs? Should I say I dropped some money? (My excuse for Miss Cooper yesterday.) Should I say I've been exercising? (Do I *look* the exercising type?) Running up and down to get rid

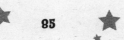

of cramp? (I'd be more likely to lie on the sofa groaning pitifully.) Testing the steps for a health and safety project at school? (Get *real*, Sadie. . .)

"Hi!" said Cormac, appearing above me in his non-funeral, out-of-hours uniform of jeans and a T-shirt. The late afternoon sun was directly behind him, making a golden halo of light around his red head of hair.

Help. He looked like an avenging angel (in Levi's), sent by God to protect the souls below from small devil children armed with cameras and morbid curiosity.

Which made a thought ping into my stressed-out brain. Dealing with death all the time, was Cormac's family hyper-religious, maybe? Was the flat upstairs as bleak as me and Hannah had joked, only with a smattering of crucifixes around the place and a copy of the Bible beside *Funerals Today* magazine on the coffee table?

Forget the flat. Think of an excuse. Think of one now, I ordered myself.

"Hey, I've got a DVD of your dad's – I've been meaning to give it back for ages," said Cormac, moving out of a direct beam of sunshine so that he suddenly looked less like an angel and more like a normal, kind-of-gangly, seventeen-year-old boy. A boy who didn't seem even remotely interested in asking about all the stomping, metallic racket I'd apparently been making. "You want to come up and get it?"

He waved a DVD with comedian Eddie Izzard on it.

"Uh, sure!" I nodded.

I took my first step on to the flight of stairs that went upwards. Strangely, my legs felt they were filled with custard, while my chest felt like there was a tiny, runaway horse let loose in there.

The stress of nearly getting caught 'cause of Harry plus the excitement of noseying at the flat upstairs *might* just make me keel over, I worried.

Yikes – I wasn't in a fit state to meet Cormac's brother while on the brink of a *coma*.

I willed my legs to get a grip of themselves and carried on upwards.

Here goes, here goes, here goes!

Oh. . .

Glitz versus Gloomy . . .

Double oh.

Actually, it was more of a "Whoah!!"

I'd convinced myself to expect lots of matt-black and chrome, and maybe white or pale grey walls. I'd expected minimal home comforts, and maybe a random bit of untidiness (it was a flat where two lads lived, after all).

I hadn't really expected . . . any of *this*. Any of the colour, and the brightness and the, well, *stuff*.

"Sorry. Should have warned you to shield your eyes!" Cormac smiled awkwardly at me, as if he was worried I might faint from kitsch-overload.

"Wow. . ." I mumbled, dropping the sarcasm (temporarily) as I gazed round at the red walls, the black chandelier, the gold-sprayed grandad clock, and the collection of chunky, multi-coloured glass vases on the mantelpiece.

Then there was the yellow egg-shaped plastic

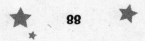

88

chair, the fake cowhide rug, a desk with a big mirror attached, framed by bulbs (showbiz dressing-room style), and three absolutely *huge* silvered prints.

I still had my camera clutched in my hand. I wished I was bolshy enough to ask to take pictures. Hannah would never *believe* this place. . .

"That's Marlene Dietrich, an old actress," Cormac began to explain, spotting what I was looking at and pointing towards the prints. "That's Catherine Deneuve, a famous French actress, and that's Twiggy—"

"She was the Kate Moss of the 1960s, wasn't she?" I jumped in, recognizing the face of the one-time most famous model in the world.

"Yeah. They're some of my brother's pin-ups," said Cormac, nodding at these icons with heads blown up ten times bigger than ours. These prints were the sort of thing you'd expect to see in glamorous West End galleries or something. Not in a funeral director's top-floor flat in the less hip side of Highbury, North London.

A giant gilt mirror reflected my stunned expression back at me. "Kyle got those pictures from a client he was working with," Cormac went on.

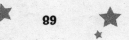

What – someone was so skint that they paid for their grandad's funeral in *art*?

"But Kyle's mad on collecting, anyway. He's really into retro furniture and whatever," said Cormac, pulling a face as he indicated the brown and burnt orange, swirly-patterned, L-shaped sofa as an example.

"Oh," I said, feeling slightly seasick just looking at it.

"He got that from the Stables Market in Camden. He says it's a twentieth-century design classic, and that it'll be worth *loads* one day."

I didn't know about it being worth loads. Worth sticking in a *skip*, maybe.

"Should have seen the looks we got when we took it home in the back of the hearse. . ."

"The *hearse*? Were your parents all right with that?" I asked. It didn't sound like a fantastic idea to let the public see a skanky old sofa stuffed where coffins are meant to be lying in rest.

"They didn't know – Kyle just sort of 'borrowed' the keys and roped me in to help. But Dad went *mental* when he found out!"

"How *did* he find out?"

"The florist down the road who does most of the wreaths for our funerals – Kyle drove right by her shop. So of course she mentioned it to Dad."

"Uh-oh. So what did your dad do?" I asked, expecting the answer to be along the lines of threatening Kyle with the sack.

"He nearly threw him out of the flat!" said Cormac. "Kyle was in a total panic. My parents own the whole building, and Kyle would never normally be able to afford a flat as big as this. He'd have had to get rid of half of his things!"

We both looked round again. I hadn't spotted the suspended mirror ball and the dressmaker's dummy wearing what looked like a knitted suit of armour.

"But your dad calmed down about it?" I asked, wondering where exactly (and *why* exactly) you'd buy a knitted suit of armour.

"Well, Mum calmed him down. She got Kyle to apologize like crazy and so Dad let him off with it in the end. Mum was pretty relieved; she's got a huge soft spot for Kyle, and she thinks all his stuff here is just amazing."

"I guess," I found myself muttering out loud, as I stared and stared. "I suppose I just didn't think your brother would be into this . . . this kind of thing."

"Huh?" Cormac blinked at me, all of a sudden slightly confused. "But you haven't met him yet, have you?"

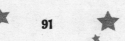

"*No* – I just mean that . . . I wouldn't have thought an undertaker would've been into this sort of look."

I could practically see Cormac's mind whirling, trying to figure out what I'd just said. Still, *what* was so hard to understand?

"But Gerry didn't choose anything in here," he said finally.

Now it was *my* turn to be confused – it felt like we were suddenly talking in two different languages.

"I thought you said your brother's name was *Kyle?*" I ventured, hoping that came out as English, and not a little-known dialect from a remote part of Mongolia.

"I've got *two* older brothers – Kyle's twenty-four and Gerry's twenty-six," said Cormac, starting to make a little sense. "*Gerry's* the undertaker. He lives in Stroud Green with his wife and kid."

"Oh . . . so Kyle *isn't?*"

"Working in the family business? *No!*" Cormac started to laugh, as if the idea of this Kyle slipping on a black suit and being respectfully mournful was the dumbest idea ever. "Kyle's a make-up artist. He works on video shoots and ad campaigns and stuff like that."

"What, you mean music videos?" I asked, intrigued.

"Yeah, that kind of thing," Cormac said matter-of-factly.

Was it matter-of-factly? Or was it more *wearily*? He'd just said that their mum had a soft spot for this Kyle, which sounded more than a little bit familiar to me.

"Do you ever. . ." I tried to think how to phrase what had just popped into my head. "I mean, do you get fed up with people thinking your brother's life is all glitzy, while yours is more . . . gloomy?"

I shouldn't have said gloomy. I hadn't meant to make Cormac sound like he was a close relative of Eeyore.

"People can think what they like," he said, his smile slipping away as he reached out to pass me Dad's DVD. "What about you, Sadie – do you ever feel second-best compared to Sonny?"

Cormac could have meant that in a genuinely concerned way, OR it could've been a dig, since I'd just made his life sound as depressing as a dose of diarrhoea.

I decided to take it the second way.

"Of course not!" I lied, snatching the DVD from him.

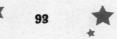

I bet he knew that translated as a big, fat "yes".

Feeling my face start to flush as red as the walls, I muttered something about having to get the tea started for Dad and stomped off towards the fire escape, my head held high.

Giving Cormac a fantastic view of my bizarrely grazed chin.

Great.

Now he could come up with a new comedy routine about me, trying to guess a ton of weird ways for a person to get carpet burns in that exact spot. . .

10

Dead rock stars and cat crunchies

"Sonny"
"Kennedy"
"Marcus"
"Hal"
"Ziggy"

The cavernous theatre was in darkness.

Except for the stage, of course.

Bathed in soft, muted spotlights, the five members of the band stood with their (glittering) backs to the audience, waiting for the clapping and cheering to die down.

But *I* wasn't clapping or cheering. In fact, anyone sitting in the row behind me probably thought they'd accidentally wandered onto the set of a horror movie: I must've looked like I was slowly being swallowed alive by my seat, the way I was slinking lower, lower, lower and groaning softly, softly, softly. . .

But I was actually just hunkering down from the sheer shame of seeing my brother's name displayed in diamanté on the back of his black biker jacket, same as the other lads. How naff was *that*? You'd never have got Kurt Cobain – the lead singer of Nirvana, officially the Coolest Rock Band in the History of Rock Bands – swaggering on stage with a jacket that twinkled "*Kurt*" on the back.

Urgh.

I wished Mum and Will and Dad hadn't made me come.

"Ladies and gentleman, boys and girls," a voice boomed out over the audience (Benny's? It sounded like him), "please put your hands together for the newest pop sensation!! Welcome, *SADIE ROCKS. . .!*"

Another roar of cheering, another mortified slink down into my seat.

As my elbows clunked against the armrests, I realized I had my hands slapped across my face, peering through the fingers. And through those comforting gaps I could see the boys in the band turn round to face their audience.

Oh.

That was weird.

They all had red eyes. Not *eyeshadow* – I mean

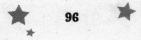

eyes. Like that red-eye effect you get sometimes in flash photos, where your smiling Auntie June suddenly looks less like your favourite, kind auntie and more like a psycho zombie serial killer. Was this some other dumb image idea that Benny had come up with? Get Sonny and Kennedy and everyone to stick in coloured contact lenses? Well, from where *I* was sitting (very low down), it didn't seem the *greatest* idea in the world, not when your target market was little school kids and their doting mummies and daddies and grandparents. I'd have thought wholesome and nice and smiley was a better look. Having a poster on your wall of five boys who looked like psycho zombie serial killers could give little kids nightmares, for goodness' sake.

And speaking of smiles, why didn't they try it? The mean and moody stares the boys were giving out didn't really match the nauseating titles of the songs I knew they'd got so far: "You – You're My Best Friend", "Hey! Let's Dance!!" and "A Hundred Hugs".

I mean, right this second, I couldn't see any small fan thinking of Sonny, Kennedy and whatever-their-names-were as best friends they might want to dance along with. Let alone *hug*. (Run away from, more like. Or call the police about.)

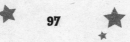

Y'know, the lack of smiling was seriously freaky in Sonny's case. Like I said before, he was normally a walking grin-machine. He was obviously a better actor than I realized; his glaring, scarlet-eyed frown was giving me goosebumps. . .

But OK – something was happening now. In one sudden movement, all the boys in the band lifted their left arms, raising their microphones to their mouths.

"Hi," they all purred, in perfect harmony. And as they "hi"d, they all broke into smiles, giant grins that revealed . . . *fangs*.

"Mum," I said suddenly, pushing out my elbow to nudge her next to me, "I'm not sure I li—"

I stopped as my elbow touched, well, *nothing*. Whipping my head around, I saw red velvet seat after red velvet seat along my row, all *empty*.

In fact, every seat on this side of the theatre was empty! Where had they all disappeared to?!

In a panic, I turned round to Dad – who wasn't there either. Though *his* seat wasn't empty.

"All right?" asked Kurt Cobain, stopping scooping ice cream from the tub he was holding to flash me a fanged smile. . .

And that's when I woke up with a boink.

The boink was Clyde, hopping on the bed and

gazing at me with liquid brown eyes and a slightly snarly expression, which was a lot nicer than the vampire rock star in my bad dream.

"Hey, glad to see you!" I said softly, scratching and stroking at his velvety ears.

Clyde wasn't supposed to come into our bedrooms, but that didn't stop him trying. I wasn't used to the stiffness of my new bedroom door (Sonny's old bedroom door), and hadn't shoved it shut hard enough to withstand a determined rabbit head-butt. But I was pretty grateful for this midnight visitation, since my nightmare had been about as much fun as falling for one of Harry's practical jokes.

Plus I might have lain here all night with the light on, the book I'd been reading flopped open on my chest, and the glass of water I'd been drinking from tipped against my leg, trickling cold water over my thighs every time I flinched (and there'd probably been a lot of flinching going on in the last few minutes, considering I was at quite possibly the first ever vampire boy-band concert – in my head, at least).

Three minutes later, I'd changed into clean – and more importantly *dry* – pyjama bottoms, put the book and the nearly empty glass on my bedside table, and snuggled up to sleep with Clyde.

Thirty minutes later, I was still wide awake, not used to the spotlight of moon spilling in through my thin curtains. (On the other side of the house, my bedroom had faced the street, where the golden-orange glow of the street light usually seeped into my room. It was like going to sleep in a can of Tango, which was quite soothing, if you want to know.)

"Great. First I had a nightmare, and now I've got insomnia," I said to Clyde, scooping him up off my bed. "Fancy a midnight snack?"

Clyde wrinkled his nose a bit, which I took to be a yes.

And so five-and-a-half minutes later, we were sitting on the living-room carpet with Dog under the soft beam of the table lamp, eating Marmite on toast, lettuce and cat food.

"What do you think my dream meant?" I asked Dog.

Dog was probably mulling over my question, but hiding it well by wolfing down the extra bowl of cat crunchies I'd just stuck in her cage.

Even though I'd banished the spooks out of my head with toast and a big glass of strawberry-flavoured milk (served with two stripy straws for extra cheerfulness), I couldn't quite get over the weirdness of my dream.

I guessed it had been triggered by the conversation with Cormac the day before, when I was in his weird and wonderful flat. And then I'd dozed off while I was reading, with thoughts of being second-best to Sonny lurking in the back of my head, which led – shazam! – to my subconscious dragging out those thoughts, going berserk with them, and turning my brother's band into the main characters of a horror movie, with an audience of one (me). If you don't count a fantasy, fanged, dead rock star, of course.

"What did you say?" I asked Dog, through a last, bulging mouthful of Marmite. I leant closer, as if I was listening intently to her advice.

Dog carried on eating, her plastic lampshade collar plinking awkwardly off the edge of the bowl.

"Huh? You think I need to find something to be good at, so I don't feel second-best any more?" I answered myself.

(Thank goodness no one was around to see me acting so goofy. I'd *never* live it down.)

"So what sort of thing?" I asked out loud, unclicking the lock on the big cage, so I could continue my conversation at close quarters, while giving my lonesome, incarcerated cat a cuddle.

I waved at Clyde to come and join us, but he

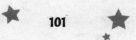

just looked at me, and hopped away, taking his lettuce leaf with him.

"Well, *I* was thinking I could be a music journalist, and then write really terrible reviews of Sonny's band. What d'you reckon?"

Dog probably reckoned I was a bit to big to be sitting in her cage, since my knees were under my chin and I'd just narrowly avoided resting my hand in the litter tray.

"Or maybe I could be a band manager, and get a rival *indie* band together. A *girl* indie band," I decided, now wide awake with possibilities.

The only sound in response was the plink of plastic on ceramic, and the gentle crunch of lettuce from somewhere behind the sofa.

"Or maybe I could open a really successful chain of record shops – and ban Sonny's CDs!"

Ten minutes later, I'd rattled through as many anti-Sonny careers as I could think of. This general stupidness was quite a fun, middle-of-the-night, boredom-busting pastime, so I decided that maybe I should carry on, but just diversify a bit.

"OK – so how about this: I *could* work on this insomnia thing," I muttered, feeling more wide awake than I ever did in the daytime, especially during geography lessons. "Maybe I could train myself to stay awake for *days*, and get into the record books!"

Ha.

I was destined to be a failure at record-breaking insomnia too. 'Cause the next thing I remembered was the sound of Martha's giggly gurgling and Will's puzzled voice saying my name.

"Sadie? What are you doing in there? Were you asleep?"

Asleep, cold and in pain.

I tried to sit up, but half a night spent snoozing while folded up like a penknife had made every joint and muscle seize up. Plus the cat crunchies embedded in my left cheek weren't too comfortable either.

"I'm fine," I lied. "Just came down to see Dog. Only been here five minutes."

"Oh . . . cool!" said Will, nodding as if he believed me (though the frowning blond eyebrows gave him away).

Cool. . . Will should get that word copyrighted, he (over) used it so much.

Anyway, this situation was the opposite of cool © (copyright Will); this was most definitely *un*-cool © (copyright *me*).

"Just going to jump in the shower," I mumbled,

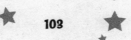

backing gingerly out of the cage, while Dog thumped herself against my face in as close an attempt to give me a cat-love-rub as she could manage in a giant plastic collar.

Boy, did I need a shower. Not just to warm up my stiff, cold body, but to get the smell of used cat litter out of my hair (*please* let me be wrong in thinking I'd used the litter tray as a pillow during the night).

"Sorry – Sonny's beaten you to it!" said Will, holding a wriggling, squiggling Martha in his arms. "Heard him practising his scales in there when we passed, so he could be a while!"

Fantastic.

I was even second-best to Sonny when it came to equal rights to the shower. . .

The rose-tinted specs effect

"What about *this* one?" asked Dad.

Da-da-da, da-da-da, da-da-da, da-da-da...
THUD-THUD-THUD-da-DA-da-THUD-THUD-
THUD-da-DA-da...

I frowned for a second, trying to place the tune he was thumping on the edge of the table with the palms of his hands.

"I've got it!!" I said suddenly. "It's "Jean Jeanie", by David Bowie!"

Even though it was a pretty ancient song (from the 1970s, I think), it hadn't been *that* hard to guess, since "Jean Jeanie" was one of Dad's Top Ten Tracks Of All Time.

So how come he was thumping it out on a table top in the Iznik café, at 5.30 p.m. on a Thursday night? Well, me and Sonny were going to have an out-of-the-blue tea with Dad (he'd texted earlier, when he'd had some good news at work and felt like celebrating). And while we waited for Sonny to show up (he was at yet more after-school band rehearsals), Dad and I were playing the Intro Game.

The way you play it is like this: first you need a partner (i.e. Dad), then you think of the beginning of a song, and drum it on the nearest surface till the other person guesses what it is. Then you swap.

It was fun – though perhaps not for the people sitting at the next table to us, or the waitress scooting back and forward, giving us irritated sideways glances. They'd all suffered through half a dozen or so intros so far, and didn't look like they could handle too many more.

"Your turn!" said Dad, nodding at me, and helping himself from the bowl of olives the waitress had just dumped down beside us.

"Nah. We'd better stop. I think there are people in here who want to kill us."

Dad looked a little puzzled for a second (I'm the child of two air-heads – where did I get my black humour from?), so I felt like I'd better explain.

"The drumming is annoying people!" I whispered, bending across the table and the bowl of olives to be heard.

"Really?" said Dad, running a hand through his

sandy coloured hair, which was resembling an Elvis Presley-style quiff more and more as the weeks went by. The long sideburns didn't help. *Please* let him never dye it black. . .

"Yes, *really*!" I hissed.

Dad was bemused. Music was as important to him as food, air and sleep (and ice-cold beer, perhaps). He could never get the fact that most other people weren't as nuts about music as him. To his way of thinking, Dad might have expected the other customers of the café to join in at the sound of the drumming, by happily whistling along or tapping their forks on their glasses. The fact that they were more likely to want to *throw* a fork at his head was beyond him.

"Wow. . ." he muttered softly, absently drumming his fingers on the table.

I put my hand over his to get him to stop.

Mum, of course, was just as mad about music as Dad – only a totally different kind of music. I think she must have seemed such an exotic creature to Dad when they first got together. I mean, here was this pretty, dark-haired girl who was besotted by composers he'd hardly even heard of. Maybe he thought she'd open the door on a whole new type of music that he'd never been into before. But it didn't happen. . . Dad tried and tried to get his head around Bartok and Shostakovich but, really, he just wanted to get back to bands with stupid names like Echo and the Bunnymen and The Teardrop Explodes.

In the end, I think it was like that sort of language problem me and Cormac had yesterday, when we were speaking about two different brothers at the same time. Maybe my parents would still be together if they'd had a translator. . .

"So, what's this new contract thing you've got?" I asked Dad, trying to sound interested in his work.

Look, it's not like I'm some ungrateful daughter who doesn't give a hoot about what their parents do for a job. It's just that it's *very* hard to get excited about paper plates (*and* paper bags *and* paper napkins *and* plastic cutlery *and* all the rest of the – let's face it, unthrilling – paper and plastic goods my dad sells from his small warehouse unit a few streets from here).

"Oh, just a new restaurant that's opening up," Dad replied, sounding about as unthrilled as I was. I guess when your dream job would've been to play bass guitar with The Jam circa 1980, being a paper-plate salesman is a bit of a letdown. Though he has his moments; when I dropped by

Dad's work after school today, he and the guys who work for him – Daryl and Kemal – were having a spin-the-plate competition.

"That's nice," I said with a big grin, confusing him again. Dad must have thought I was ridiculously and unnecessarily pleased about the restaurant contract, when really I was just smiling at the thought of him shouting "Hoopla!!" as he spun a Disney Princess paper plate in the air on top of a broom handle.

"Your chin's looking much better today," he said, tilting his own chin up, as if I needed reminding what he was talking about.

I'd shown Dad and Gran my Harry war wound over tea at his place last night. Gran had insisted on finding some miracle healing cream from the chemist shop's-worth of toiletries and medicines she'd stocked up Dad's bathroom cabinet with.

"Thanks," I said, glad to know that I didn't need to go out and buy a fake beard to cover up the carpet burn with after all.

"Oh, and that reminds me – you left this at mine," added Dad, pulling my silver camera out of his jacket pocket. "Got any good shots on there?"

"Nope," I said hurriedly, in case he was hinting at a viewing to pass the time till Sonny got there.

I mean, there were lots of funny and cute

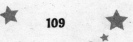

photos on the memory stick (me, Hannah and Letty in our painting pyjamas; Martha draped in nasturtiums), but considering that the last two frames were of a) a passing hearse, and b) the back window of McConnell & Sons Funeral Directors, as snapped by horrid Harry, I preferred that Dad didn't see them. *Just* in case he thought I was turning into as much of a morbid weirdo as Harry evidently was.

Tried 2 tell Mum wot H had been up 2 at yr Dad's – but she was 2 tired and not really listening, Hannah had texted me earlier today. It was pretty tough for her; she could tell her parents that Harry had sold their house and bought a sweet factory with the proceeds, and they'd just act like he was a funny toddler getting up to innocent mischief, instead of a ten-year-old practical-joke terrorist.

It's the rose-tinted specs effect: same as Mum and Dad have with Sonny. They think they treat us exactly the same, but they absolutely *don't.*

Course, maybe it was slightly *my* fault. Maybe I should just learn to incessantly talk at high speed and high volume. But I'd find that pretty hard to do, since I'm not a *nerk.*

"SORRY! DIDN'T THINK I'D BE SO LATE!!" someone called out loudly, causing everyone in the Iznik to spin round. "I TRIED TO CALL BUT MY PHONE'S OUT OF CREDIT!"

Sigh. . .

See? *Normal* people who were running late would hurry into a café, come right up to the people they were meeting, and then give their apologies in a *normal* speaking voice.

Whereas *Sonny* had to proclaim his lateness from the doorway of the café, projecting his voice like he was on the stage of a West End theatre without a microphone. (Yes, they could hear you at the back: right at the back of the kitchen!)

"That's OK!" said Dad, kicking a chair out for Sonny to sit down on. "Rehearsals running late again?"

"Are you wearing make-up?" I interrupted, before Sonny could launch into an elaborate answer. It was just that the way he was looking was spooking me out. It made him seem sort of hyper-real, just like he'd been in my dream last night. At least now there was no sign of diamanté, red-eye or fangs. Just a lot of foundation and a flick of mascara. . .

"I go to a *theatre* school, remember!" Sonny said to me, trying to sound all brightly sarcastic. "There *are* times at theatre school when you're going to have to wear stage make-up!"

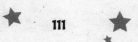

"Yeah, but you don't have to wear it out in the *street*," I pointed out, casually popping an olive in my mouth.

Stumped, Sonny turned away from me and started talking to Dad instead.

"No, it wasn't the rehearsals that made me late. It was just that Benny *really* needed to talk to us all after we'd finished. He said he had something to tell us. . ."

Sonny paused for dramatic effect. I refused to play into his hands and seem interested, and sucked the last of my fizzy water noisily through a straw instead.

"And what did Benny say?" asked Dad, intrigued.

"He said. . ." sighed Sonny, "that he can't take the band on this bonding exercise on Sunday after all!"

"What, the Cowboys and Indians thing?" I interjected, using the most bored voice I could muster.

"It's based on young *Native American* warrior rituals, remember?" said Sonny, shooting a glare my way.

Yeah, young Native American rituals that had probably been made up by a hippy from Croydon who wanted to cash in on mugs like Benny and his pop protégées.

"So what's the problem? Why can't he take you any more?" Dad asked.

"Well, there's this big, important drama festival going on at the South Bank Centre this weekend. . ." Sonny started to explain.

The South Bank Centre is down by the River Thames, beside the London Eye. It's this fairly ugly bunch of concrete buildings that house amazing theatres and stuff. Plus there are always heaps of bizarre outdoor street theatre things going on, as well as buskers and whatever on the Thames footpath, right outside the buildings. It's a pretty amazing place to hang out, if you're ever in central London.

"It turns out that Benny's an understudy for an actor taking part in the drama festival, and he just heard that this actor guy broke his leg, so Benny's going to have to do it."

"Mmm, it must be hard to be a living statue when you've got a broken leg. . ." I muttered.

Sadly, I'd muttered my excellent joke a bit too quietly. Sonny had already started talking over me, filling Dad in with more unnecessary detail.

"Benny would have tried to get out of it, 'cause he's totally committed to the band now, but he had put his name down for this and it wouldn't have been professional to pull out."

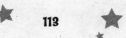

"Right, right. . ." Dad was nodding earnestly. "I can see that."

I scooped up three olives, wedged them between my top lip and my teeth, and examined my reflection in the back of a spoon. (Well, I had to indulge in a bit of boredom-busting now that I knew – from experience – that I'd been more-or-less excluded from this conversation.)

"We're all gutted," said Sonny, looking very, very gutted indeed. That expression would come in handy if he ever got a part as a patient in a hospital drama, and was told his leg had to be amputated or something. "We were *really* looking forward to it."

"Tell you what!" said Dad, rat-a-tatting his hands on the table, like he was getting everyone's attention for an announcement. "Give me Benny's number – *I* could take all of you lads!"

I stopped dead, just as I was distractedly squashing a fourth and fifth olive under my top lip. I was suddenly caught out by the image of my dad in his Hawaiian shirt, sitting in a teepee trying to *chant*. He'd never even manage to get his legs in a crossed position without huffing and swearing.

"It's too late – Benny phoned his friend at the retreat to cancel. He said his mate was cool about

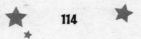

it, 'cause there's always a waiting list of people dying to do it," Sonny said sorrowfully.

"Well, forget the Native American ritual . . . thingy!" exclaimed Dad, waving his hand over the table. "I'm sure I can come up with something that would be a great bonding experience for you guys!"

"*Yeah!!*" said Sonny, his eyes all alight, as if Dad had just announced, "We'll put the show on right here!"

I half-expected a troupe of break-dancers to burst out of the kitchen and leap on the tables, doing head spins and windmills, while a soundtrack from "High School Musical" blared out of the café speakers instead of Turkish ballads.

Or maybe not.

Whatever – I felt like pointing out to my over-excited twin that Dad's idea of bonding would probably be something like taking Sonny and Kennedy and Co. on a tour of North London pub venues where Dad's favourite bands had played in. Either that, or he'd have them all geared up with Disney Princess paper plates and broom handles in a sudden-death spinning contest come Sunday morning.

"More olives?" asked the waitress.

I realized she was speaking to me, as Dad and

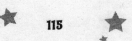

Sonny were currently locked into mobile phone chattering and number swapping.

The waitress was obviously asking because she'd noticed most of the olives from the bowl were positioned weirdly in my mouth, making me look like the Elephant Man. And she obviously meant it sarcastically.

But what the heck, it was nice to have someone paying me a bit of attention.

"Yesh, pleash," I mumbled, trying not to drool out of the corner of my mouth. . .

Small smiles and big smirks

Who knew cats liked sinks so much?

My cat Dog certainly didn't. But maybe she was missing out on a very pleasurable experience. According to the website I was currently scrolling through, sinks were a big hit with *loads* of cats; a big enough hit to have a whole website full of fluffy, gorgeous, contented-looking moggies snoozing under the hot and cold taps.

How excellently stupid.

It was also as stupid as a couple of *other* websites Hannah had emailed me the links for: one listing bizarre museums (I really, *really* wanted to check out the Carrot Museum), and one with photos of funny-shaped clouds that looked like Jesus or Mickey Mouse or broccoli or whatever.

So what was I up to, exactly? Well, I was giving my brain a break and flicking through these dumb sites 'cause the hour and a half of English

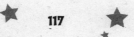

homework I'd just done had melted my mind. (Yeah, *that* and listening to Sonny droning on and on about his boring band and their dull dance moves all through tea at the Iznik. It was enough to put you off your dolmades. . .)

Downloading photos (and deleting images) from my camera had also been on my agenda this evening, but even *that* seemed too much like hard work, I was so tired. I decided I might just have a glance at one more pleasantly pointless site that Hannah had let me know about (apparently a mausoleum for a dead pet, made out of Lego) and then go to bed ridiculously early. And let's hope there'd be no vampire-boy-band nightmares tonight.

Ping!

Hurray! An email for me. Maybe it would be Letitia moaning about the homework, or then again maybe it would be Hannah letting me know about another bizarre link to a website I needed to check out absolutely *immediately*.

It turned out to be neither.

It turned out to be a bit of a surprise. Mainly 'cause it was from Sonny.

How funny that instead of walking ten steps along the first-floor landing to communicate with me, my brother had zapped a message thousands of kilometres up into the sky to a satellite bobbing about in space, and down it had come again to land in my computer. Isn't technology wonderful? Aren't my twin and me close? (*Not.*)

So what did he want? Ah . . . he wanted me to be his "friend" on something called "B-sussed:". What was that? I clicked on the link, which took me to an intro page that looked a bit like MySpace or Beebo or Facebook or one of those.

Here we go. . .

Transferring to the music section. . .

And – urgh! – filling nearly my entire screen was a snapshot of Sonny, Kennedy the human frying pan, and the other three members of the band . . . all beaming out cute 'n' corny grins, like they were begging you to like them (and of course buy their records, once they'd got around to making any). Their tutor – and I guess *manager* – Benny must have come up with the idea of launching this page. I bet he told the boys to ask all their mates and loved ones (and me) to sign up as "friends", just to make them look instantly popular.

Bah. I didn't want to be their "friend". I'd rather spend the next month sleeping in Dog's *cage* than sign up.

Or had I accidentally signed up just by clicking

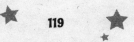

on the link in the first place, I suddenly fretted, glancing around the page for clues, and finding none.

What my gaze *did* settle on was the small bit of blurb beside the photo; what exactly did it have to say about the band?

"Coming soon – the new pop sensation, Sa—"

Ping!

More mail. I flipped on to the email icon to see who it was this time. Maybe Sonny saying he'd sent me the link by mistake?

Nope, it was . . . oh.

Someone called CMcC. Cormac McConnell.

Well, it was a certainly a strange evening, filled with cats in sinks, carrot museums and brothers trying to be friends with you (in cyberspace at least), but this email was perhaps the most unexpected thing I'd seen on my computer in the last hour.

Where had Cormac got my email address from? Sonny maybe? Or even Dad?

Hi Sadie. Did you get a request from Sonny to be a "friend" on the band's website?

"Yes," I answered him aloud, as if he could hear me. I was just a bit flummoxed, I suppose. It's weird when you come across people in different situations than you're used to. Like the time I bumped into Miss Cooper from school coming out of the showers at the local swimming pool in the smallest towel known to man (yewww. . .).

And did you get the other message from Sonny – the one about the rehearsal they're doing after school tomorrow?

"Nope," I replied out loud, with a shake of my head. *Write that, you idiot!* I scolded myself. But there was more to read first.

Sonny invited me along to watch them – he said it might help me think about my performance, when I'm doing comedy.

"Sonny is four years younger than you – don't let him be so patronizing!" I practically shouted at the screen (with the "SONNY BIRD IS A NERK" photo glimmering as the background).

I want to check it out, but not mad on going on my own. Are you going already? Or fancy coming with me?

I had a small smile, and then a big smirk to myself.

The small smile, 'cause I was pretty pleased to see Cormac and me could still be mates after bugging each other yesterday evening.

The big smirk, 'cause it could be a lot of fun to sit and watch Sonny and his mates prancing about in their awful neon and black cycling shorts. With a camera to record any choice fluffed moments in the dance routines, of *course*.

Sure! I typed back to CMcC. *I'd LOVE to come. . .*

S**** Rocks. . .

Hey, I *try* to act laidback and cool © (copyright Will).

Hopefully, most of the time I'm convincing (well, obviously *not* when I'm not falling over tripwires of string, being caught napping in a pet cage and shoving olives under my top lip).

And today – waiting for Cormac outside Sonny's stage school – I was having to bluff a whole *heap* of laidbackness and coolness.

I was nervous, OK? Nervous *of* and nervous *about*. . .

a) Meeting up with Cormac, since I'd never hung out with him without Dad or Sonny around (unless you included our spiky conversation in his brother's bling!-y Bachelor Pad the other day)

b) Sonny being grouchy with me for turning up at his band rehearsal (I hadn't said anything

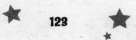

to him about coming – just thought I'd leave it as a "lovely" surprise)

c) All the various confident and bright-looking stage-school students ambling in and out of the entrance to the building (you could tell it wasn't *my* school, where everyone would be out of the premises like a shot, half a minute after the end-of-day bell had fired off).

Anyway, as I stood and waited for Cormac, I adopted a very casual – though slightly uncomfortable – slouch, in the hope that I didn't stand out like a sore (non-stage-school) thumb.

"C'mon, c'mon, c'mon. . ." I mumbled under my breath, glancing both ways along the street in search of Cormac. "Where are you?"

Sonny had told Cormac that the rehearsal would start at 4 p.m. It was ten-past already. If Cormac didn't turn up soon then I was in severe danger of losing my bottle and skulking off home, without seeing Sonny and his buddies "perform". And where would be the fun in that?

I concentrated on looking left. I figured Cormac would be most likely to come from that direction, as the road eventually led to Upper Street, and the natural way he might be walking from Highbury.

Which is why I *wasn't* looking when a sleek black hearse pulled up beside me from the right.

"Hi, Sadie! Sorry I'm late – couldn't get away from a funeral!" Cormac garbled, clambering out of the passenger side door. I was relieved to see that there were no dead passengers in the car (the coffin-cum-sofa-transporting back section was empty). There was, of course, someone pretty much alive in the driver's seat, and an older, brown-haired version of Cormac gave me a quick smile and a wave as he smoothly pulled away into the traffic again.

"Is that your brother Gerry, then?" I asked.

"Yep!" said Cormac, pink-cheeked from rushing, and now pulling his black tie off. "So, do you know which way to go?"

"Sure, I've been here loads of times," I said, like the place was my second home.

In truth, I'd only been here a handful of times, to see end-of-term shows with Mum, Dad, Will, Gran and Martha, or any combination of those. The last show had been some very eco thing set in a future world that had been ravaged by dumb earthlings who'd paid no attention to green issues. It would've been good, I think, except that I knew every line word perfect since Sonny had been practising the script twenty-seven hours a day, eight days a week in the run-up to it.

"We just go in the main door here," I said, leading the way.

After the main door, unfortunately, I wasn't sure where I was going. Still, this person at the desk would be able to help. Or maybe she'd ask us to leave, sensing a whiff of fakeness about us. We were non-performing strangers, after all, and had no right to be here.

"Well, hello! How can I help?" beamed the receptionist. (It was freaky; everyone to do with this place was always so unnaturally happy.)

"Uh, yes," I said, drumming my fingers on the desk (like father, like daughter). "Which way for the. . . um, *mumble-mumble* rehearsal?"

Help. I was finding it impossible to say the band name out loud. Actually, I couldn't even write it down. I'd come to a compromise and typed it as "S**** Rocks. . ." on an email to Hannah last night, telling her what I was up to today.

"What, sorry?" asked the receptionist, turning her head to hear me better.

"The band Sadie Rocks," Cormac jumped in. "We got invited along to watch their rehearsal."

"By Sonny Bird. He's my brother," I chipped in too.

"Oh, yes, of course. Wow, you *are* alike!" beamed the receptionist.

"Worse luck!" I joked, though I wasn't really joking.

"Ha, ha! Well, just sign in here . . . take these visitor badges . . . and go down the corridor till you see a sign on the right for Dance Studio Three!"

And so we signed, we clipped our badges on, and were very soon slipping into a frighteningly brightly-lit studio, with a large bunch of people (other stage-school students by the look of them) lounging on the shiny wooden floors, and a small bunch of people (Sonny and his buddies) kneeling or crouched down at the far end.

Some of the larger group turned to see who just walked in, and then just looked away again, uninterested (phew). The smaller group were too busy huddled in a circle around Mr Cheesy Handsome Benny to pay us any attention (double phew).

"Let's sit down," I whispered to Cormac, yanking him down to the floor by the cuff of his suit jacket.

"Oh. . .!" Cormac muttered in what sounded like horror, as he tried to fold his long legs into a crossed position.

The band had just broken out of their circle, and were bounding to their feet. I'd forgotten that Cormac wouldn't have seen their fetching stage outfits yet.

And yeww . . . what a vision. Any future fans of the band would be immediately put off by what *I'd* just seen: Kennedy doing a sort of froggy movement and yanking around at his cycling shorts as if an escaped hamster had got in there.

The poor guy looked like he would've given anything to be dressed in a pair of baggy combats instead of skin-tight Lycra.

"Is *that* what they're going to be wearing?" asked Cormac, stretching his neck a little to gawp over the tops of the heads of the makeshift audience.

"Oh yes," I whispered, searching around in my bag for a certain something.

"Hey, everyone!" Benny suddenly called out.

"Hey!" lots of people in the audience called back. (I shrank down, as I saw Sonny grin broadly around, spotting his various mates lounging in the crowd.)

"Thanks for sticking around after classes today to be our audience," Benny continued. "The guys are just going to be practising some dance moves today, to a rough recording of one of their songs. It's called 'You – You're My Best Friend'."

A round of applause. Not from me – I was still rifling in my bag.

But gazing up, I could see five heads suddenly bowed down, as if they were in prayer. The start of their dance routine, obviously. It would have looked quite striking, if Kennedy hadn't still been fidgeting a bit, trying to get comfy in those shorts.

Meanwhile, Benny took a few steps back and pressed a button on a CD player. "A-five, six, seven, *eight*!"

Whoah! And off they went, hunching shoulders and harmonizing; body-popping and pulling poses.

People in the audience started whooping and clapping along to the track – it sounded like it was trying to be hip-hop, only it was being played on something that sounded like a pretty basic keyboard, so it didn't exactly come across as too "street".

Three minutes' worth of all-singing, all-dancing energy blasted off in front of us. The singing was OK-ish, the dancing was good, even though some of the moves were a bit corny, and then . . . then came the finale.

BOOF! – each of the five boys jumped up in the air, kicking one leg in front, kung fu style.

The effect was, um, truly awesome. Only perhaps not in the way they meant it to be. . .

"Did you get it? *Tell* me you got it!" said Cormac, as the audience cheered and groaned at the same time.

"I got it!" I grinned, lowering my camera and showing him the shot of S**** Rocks in mid-air, *just* as the seams of Kennedy's overtight shorts split wide open. (*Please* tell me those weren't Spiderman pants!)

"I've *got* to write that down," laughed Cormac, scrabbling for a little notepad in his suit pocket.

Well, Sonny had invited Cormac along today to get tips on performance, but instead he'd unexpectedly helped him get some excellent new material for his comedy act.

Uh-oh.

Seemed like the flash of the camera had unexpectedly drawn Sonny's attention to me.

"Hi!" I mouthed, raising my eyebrows and wiggling my fingers in a cheeky hello, as the whole dance studio rocked with laughter around me. . .

Blackmailing made easy

Things that me and my twin brother have in common. . .

- Mum and Dad (only they're virtually never in the same room together these days)
- Martha (awww. . .)
- The same-ish face (like looking in the mirror, and seeing a boy . . . and a nerk)
- The same-ish lopsided smile (only his looks soppy and mine looks snarly)
- The same mole above our upper lip (feel like putting concealer on mine some days)
- Music (rock and indie)
- A fear of the dentist (I'd just noticed Will's dental appointment reminder card on the kitchen table and felt a familiar shudder)
- *Kipper The Dog* (me and Sonny's joint favourite bedtime book, from ages 3–5)

- Cheese and ham toasties (the ultimate comfort food)

Things that me and my twin brother *don't* have in common. . .

- Everything else

I was just mulling over this piece of universal truth as I made Saturday morning breakfast.

"Daaaa, ddddaaaa, daaah-GAH!!"

In her fluffy white dressing gown, Martha looked like Mum's mini-me.

Or maybe it was more a case of Mum – in *her* white fluffy dressing gown – being Martha's *maxi-me*.

Whatever, they made a perfect mother and daughter pair. I, meanwhile, was making two cheese and ham toasties.

"Mmm, something smells good!" said Mum, smiling as she sat herself down on a chair, with Martha plopped on her lap and cooing.

"Hot salad cream!" I said, pointing to the toastie maker, and mentioning my secret, knock-out ingredient, which of course wasn't very secret, since it's what Sonny and I had demanded on our toasties from an early age.

"You must be hungry. . ." Mum commented, watching as I unclipped the lid of the machine to reveal two steaming, golden sandwiches.

"Nah – one's for Sonny."

I didn't look over, but I knew Mum would be smiling even more, chuffed that I was doing an unexpectedly good deed for my brother.

Well, the truth was, I felt kind of *bad* for him. Don't get me wrong; the photo I took of the kung fu kick and Kennedy's sudden underpants exposé was better than I thought, and would be great when I printed it out BIG (I only wished I'd had a video camera instead – I'd have made a fortune on one of those home-movie disaster TV shows).

But I wasn't Cruella de Vil – I knew it must have been a real bummer to have your first public band run-through turn into a huge school *joke*.

And so that's why I was making the toastie. I'd heard him clunking about in the shower a few minutes ago, so he'd be down any time now, and I'd have this waiting at his place at the table.

And hopefully, he'd understand that a hunk of bread, cheddar, ham and melted, sticky salad cream was *my* way of saying I sympathized. . .

"Wonder how Sonny's feeling today?" said Mum, gently lowering Martha down on to the floor so she could gurgle at Clyde, who was nibbling tentatively at a piece of kitchen roll that had landed nearby (as soon as Martha could crawl, I worried that she'd be copying him madly and assuming that she was part rabbit).

"About the same as he did last night, I suppose," I said, swapping the plates around so Sonny would get the unchipped one.

Me and Cormac had waited for Sonny yesterday, after the rehearsal.

I figured that any irritation he felt about me a) being at the rehearsal in the first place, and b) taking an incriminating photo, would be overtaken by the relief of having someone to go home with, so he wouldn't have to do the Walk Of Shame alone.

And I think he was kind of grudgingly grateful to have me and Cormac for company, since he spent the whole time dissecting every other minute of the performance – making sure *that* had been OK – before the climactic pant disaster.

I couldn't go through it all again when we got home (my head would have spontaneously combusted). So after tea, I'd left Mum and Will to listen to the horror of the rehearsal, and nipped upstairs to the sanctuary of my room, where I did my homework (well, you've got to), emailed Hannah and Letty, and danced (to Kasabian's

"Empire" – if you want to know – about seventeen times in a row, it's so good).

"Poor Sonny. . . He really puts his heart and soul into his school stuff," said Mum, running her hands through her hair, and not really thinking about what she was saying, as usual.

It's not that she wasn't allowed to commiserate with Sonny; it's more that she always seemed to be twenty times more interested in what *he* did than what *I* did. I guess it just didn't sound so exciting, knowing I'd put my heart and soul into my last French test. . .

"Mmm," I murmured in reply, taking an irritated bite out of my own steaming-hot sandwich without thinking of the consequences. Ouch.

"Your brother really gives a hundred and ten per cent to everything," she mused some more, pulling a big butterfly clip out of her dressing-gown pocket to snaffle up her bed-messy hair. She was talking in her usual day-dreamy way, as if a soundtrack of gentle Vivaldi was playing in her head at all times.

"Sho . . . sho do I, Mum," I tried to say, through a mouth that might just have third-degree burns, due to lava-hot cheese.

"Course you do," Mum answered sweetly, and

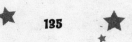

absently, the way parents do to tiny kids who say there's a tiger living under the bed.

Grrrrrr. (As tigers say, and as *I'd've* said, if I could talk with third-degree burns of the tongue.)

"By the way, what did Miss Cooper say when she gave you the permission slip to get off on Monday? Did she ask lots of questions about Sonny and the band?"

Eeeeeek!! (As tigers never say, but as *I'd've* said, if I could squeal with third-degree burns of the tongue.)

"Bit hot!" I managed to mumble, waving at my mouth and ignoring Mum's question(s).

I don't know where she thought me and my hot mouth were going, and – quite frankly – neither did I. I just needed to get away from the realization that I'd a) *not* got a permission slip to leave school early on Monday, and b) blanked the whole thing from my mind since I'd last seen Gandalf – sorry, Miss Cooper – last Tuesday.

And then inspiration struck (almost as quickly as instantaneous cheese burns) when I paused by the living-room door and saw Will on his own, flicking through Saturday morning telly programmes in search of something that wasn't CBeebies (Martha's favourite channel to gurgle at).

"Will – I need you!" I said urgently, hurtling over to join him on the sofa for a whispered conversation.

Will looked a bit scared. He liked things to be cool © (copyright Will); not mysterious and whispered.

"Uh, why?" he asked, gripping the remote control way too hard.

"You remember our little secret?"

Will knew straight away what I meant. I meant the week when Mum first went back to work after her maternity leave, leaving Will in complete charge as the home-alone dad. Will had assured her that he could look after Martha no problem, while hiding the deep, dark secret that it scared him stupid. It wasn't till I sussed him out, and got Gran onboard to teach him some basic babycare tricks of the trade, that he'd relaxed. But it had all stayed a HUGE secret from Mum, so that she didn't get herself in a tizz.

And now it was time for Will to return the favour (or risk me spilling his secret).

"Yes," he mumbled warily, accidentally switching the TV on to a shopping channel currently selling ear-splitting, shoot-'em-up computer games.

"Well, I need you to help me now," I told him,

grabbing the remote and flipping it on to a sensible channel (BBC2, showing some cooking programme), so Mum didn't hear the racket and come through and catch us in (secret) conversation.

"Help you how?" asked Will.

"Mum wrote a note to Miss Cooper, so I could get off for Sonny's contract-signing tomorrow. Only I couldn't show Miss Cooper that note, 'cause you need to have a leg hanging off or a parent dying of bubonic fever before she'll give you a permission slip to be absent!"

I was gabbling, I knew. Will was still wondering what exactly I needed him to do, I realized.

"Can you write me a letter to go with this?" I said, holding up the dental reminder card that I'd just surreptitiously swiped from the table. "If I wave this card at Ms Cooper, she won't check the time or date or notice it's for you – not if you write me a note that says I need to get off early on Monday for an urgent check-up!"

My tongue wrapped round a random tooth when I stopped talking, trying to imagine a throbbing pain there. (Hey, who said Sonny was the only actor in our family?)

"Uh . . . OK!" Will agreed, looking warily over my shoulder in case Mum was lurking within hearing distance.

"Thanks!" I said, bouncing up off the sofa so I could go give poor old Dog a bit of attention, stuck over there in her cage by the telly.

Ah, my nearly-stepdad, I thought, as I scratched Dog under the chin through the bars of her prison.

Will was so sweet, he really was. And so easy to blackmail, bless him. . . .

A weaselly weasel. . .

Like I said before, Mum always bangs on about me being the dependable, sensible, reliable twin (like that's *so* exciting), and I was currently holding a stepladder in a dependable, sensible and reliable way.

"Ah, now, we're nearly done," said Gran, with a firm note of satisfaction in her voice. "I can rest easy at last. Can I pass this down to you, Sadie, love?"

She held out a bottle of toxic spray cleaner (no germs would escape alive from Gran!), a blue and white checked cloth and a feather duster with motes of dust escaping from it in gently billowing swirls.

"Got them!" I assured her, putting her prized cleaning essentials into her special cleaning essentials plastic box under the kitchen sink. I'd have bet a hundred pounds that Dad had no idea there was a special cleaning essentials plastic box in the cupboard under the sink.

"Oh, don't tidy that away, dear – since I've got it out, I may as well do the sides of the fridge while I'm at it. . ."

Gran had phoned our house in a complete panic this morning. She had an emergency on her hands. And with Dad busy at work (on his new contract), Sonny at Saturday morning rehearsals (and not looking forward to them), and no Mum, Will or Martha around (they were hanging out at the kiddie swings in Highbury Fields), it had fallen to me (dependable, sensible, reliable Sadie) to come to her rescue.

Except that coming to her rescue did sound a bit grand for the task in hand, i.e. holding the stepladder while Gran fought the evil forces of dust and grime on top of the kitchen cabinets, armed only with yellow rubber gloves plus sheer guts and determination.

("Oh, I just couldn't sleep a *wink* last night, Sadie, love! I just realized it was the one place in the flat that I hadn't given a good scrub, and I kept thinking of all the unhygenic dirt and dust lurking up there!")

She'd love it when she finally moved back to her own house in Barnet. It would be suffering

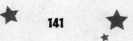

from *serious* dusting neglect and would keep her contently busy for days. Not that she seemed to be in a hurry to get back there anytime soon; she was very much settled in her prison cell at Dad's.

Ding-dong!

Saved by the bell.

I'd phoned Hannah on the way to Gran's asking her if she wanted to come meet me at Dad's. I loved my gran very much, but knew she'd somehow rope me in for more housework duties if I stayed around too long (she thinks cleaning is fun, same as Will – they're both deranged). So I'd arranged for Hannah to whisk me away from smells of bleach and Mr Sheen and go shopping, eating or mooching instead.

"The intercom thingy's not working, Sadie, love," said Gran, as I went to press the buzzer by the door.

"Oh. OK! Right – I've got to go, Gran. That's going to be Hannah for me," I said, giving her a kiss on the cheek before grabbing my bag off the kitchen doorknob.

"Ah, thanks a million for helping me out, sweetheart," Gran called out after me. "And don't do anything I wouldn't!"

"I promise!" I called back, before closing the

front door to the flat behind me.

I knew for a fact that Gran would never get a tattoo ("What a thing to do to yourself!"), eat sushi ("Raw fish! Have you ever heard of such nonsense!") or go bungee-jumping ("It could make your eyes pop out, surely!"). As I had no plans to do any of those things in the next hour or two with Hannah, I felt pretty secure about keeping my word.

"Hi. . .! Oh."

I'd thundered down the stairs as fast as my Converse trainers would carry me, and pulled open the main door, expecting to see Hannah on the pavement, waiting impatiently for me – but there was no one.

"Hannah?" I called out, looking this way and that, up and down Blackstock Road. The main door clicked closed behind me.

"*HANNAH?*"

"Hello!"

My friend's head popped out sideways from the open door of McConnell & Sons, her long dark hair hanging like a curtain.

"What are you doing in there?" I hissed at her, walking towards her a little tentatively. I mean, what was she up to? You can't just go wandering into an undertaker's, the way you might into a newsagent's when you want a nosey at the latest mags.

Undertaker's were for grieving, recently bereaved people, not thirteen-year-old girls in sparkly Led Zepplin T-shirts.

"It's OK – Cormac said we could come in for a minute," she replied, with a strange expression on her face that I couldn't quite place.

I glanced inside the shopfront, and saw through the glass window the reason for Hannah's strange expression – and the reason she said "we".

'Cause there was Cormac, talking to *Harry*.

"Mum had to cover someone else's shift at the hospital again this morning," she said hurriedly. "I was going to phone you and warn you but. . ."

But I would probably have told her not to bother coming, if I'd known her weasel of a little brother would be tagging along too.

"Oh, hi, Sadie!" said Cormac, as I followed Hannah through the open doorway.

"Harry spotted Cormac opening up, and asked if he could see inside," Hannah explained, rolling her eyes at me, knowing I'd understand what a chancer Harry could be. "He told Cormac that he'd been having nightmares about dying and stuff, which of course is rubbish!"

"It's not!" said Harry, all innocence. "It's true!"

I bet it wasn't. Weaselly Harry was just full of morbid curiosity and couldn't let a chance pass to get in here.

"It's fine!" said Cormac. "People think it'll be all gloomy, so it's good to show that it's not."

I'd never dared to look beyond the windows and the ornate silk flower arrangements when I'd passed this place on the way to Dad's. But looking around this office, or waiting room, or whatever it was exactly, it didn't look gloomy at all. With its comfy sofas, peaches 'n' cream striped wallpaper and gold-framed prints of flowers, it looked a bit like the entrance hall of an expensive but slightly old-fashioned hotel. It was all right.

"Can I look in the *other* rooms?" said Harry, his eyes aglow with gruesome possibilities.

"Sorry, no. That's all private," Cormac said, letting Harry down gently.

"Dohhh!" grumbled Harry, flopping down on to one of the sofas.

"It's sort of. . . *cosier* than I thought it would be," I told Cormac, thinking of the sad people who normally sat on these very sofas. I guess the décor aimed to be soothing, which is exactly what you need when you're feeling miserable.

As that thought whisked through my head, I went to dollop my bag on the walnut desk, but

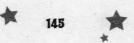

managed to miss it completely and ended up with a bunch of stuff – hairbrush, tissues, camera, mobile, half a packet of Maltesers – spilling out across the plush russet carpet.

Wow, Harry the Weasel must have been keen to make a good impression on Cormac, his new hero. I'd never have dreamt of him helping me before. But sure enough, he was on his knees quicker than Dog pouncing on her dinner, scooping up my stuff for me.

Any other time and I'd have relished the opportunity to "accidentally" step on his fingers, but in the circumstances, I couldn't exactly, could I?

"By the way, you're not waiting for anyone, are you?" I asked Cormac, suddenly worried that the reason he'd come in here was to prepare for a coffin (and its contents) to arrive any second.

"No – we're not busy today. Mum's doing some paperwork at home, and she asked me to pick up some files for her," Cormac explained. Mind you, his outfit of jeans and a blue striped T-shirt *should* have given me a clue that he wasn't working today – unless his family were trying out a revolutionary new "casual" look for the business. (Hey, instead of the black suits, maybe the new uniform could include baseball caps and butt-skimming, half-mast jeans next. . .)

"Oh, good," I said, sounding probably way too happy with his answer.

"I need the toilet!" said Harry the Weasel.

"Well, you'll just have to wait!" snapped Hannah.

"But I'm really desperate!"

"We can take him back upstairs and use the loo at Dad's," I said, softening (only very slightly) slightly towards The Weasel, since he'd done me a good deed.

"Can't wait!!! I have to go *now*!!" he whimpered, tying his legs together in complicated knots.

"It's fine – there's a loo right through here," said Cormac, walking over to a door in the back wall, and pressing a coded keypad to unlock it. "That's it there."

"Thank you!" chirped Harry, good as gold, slipping through the door that Cormac was propping open with his foot.

"Hey – I was thinking of trying out my routine in Highbury Fields again tomorrow. Do you fancy coming?"

Cormac's pale skin pinked-up as he looked at us hopefully.

"Sure!"

"Yeah, of course!"

Hannah and I spoke at once, sensing his nerves and excitement and feeling quite nervous and excited for him too. And it was pretty cool © (copyright Will) being friends with an older boy who was a stand-up comedian – even if so far he'd only ever performed standing up on a box in the local park.

"Are you going to do the same stuff this time? About Sadie, I mean?" asked Hannah.

"No – I'm going to try some other stuff out," he said with a shrug.

"Like members of boy bands ripping their trousers during energetic dance routines?" I smirked, remembering Kennedy's mortifying pants moment.

"Maybe!" Cormac smirked back. "You'll just have to come along and see!"

"Are you going to try and do your routine in comedy clubs one day?" Hannah asked.

"Well, I hope so," said Cormac, with a shy shrug. "I just have to wait till I get enough material, and enough confidence I suppose!"

"That would be great!" Hannah sighed, as if she was imagining us sitting in some crowded venue, watching our mate Cormac doing his show in the spotlight.

"No, it wouldn't! We wouldn't be able to go and see him – I'm pretty sure you have to be eighteen to get into comedy clubs!" I pointed out.

"Well, *I* wouldn't be able to perform in them either, since I'm not eighteen for another nine months!" Cormac said with a broad grin.

We all laughed for a second – then Hannah's smile flipped off like a light bulb, her face suddenly darkening.

"Harry's taking a long time. . ." she noted, peering past Cormac and towards the bathroom. "Is he still in there?"

Cormac pushed the door open – and we all saw straight away that the loo was empty.

"I bet he's trying to find the embalming room, or whatever you call it!" said Hannah in a panic.

Without thinking if we were actually allowed in that part of the premises, me and Hannah automatically rushed after Cormac, desperate to capture The Weasel before he saw something he shouldn't.

"It's OK – everything's locked up," Cormac assured us hurriedly.

And mistakenly, as it happened.

THUMP!

The noise came from a room at the end of the

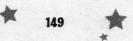

corridor – a room that we all tumbled into now. A room that was a smaller version of the soothing office outside, complete with flower arrangements, padded armchairs . . . and an open coffin.

With a little old lady in it, looking all serene and as if she was sleeping, which of course she very much *wasn't*.

I felt my chest contract at the sight of the first dead body I'd ever come across. It wasn't nearly as freaky as you might imagine. But it was still kind of . . . ugh. And wow. And *ooooooh*.

The sheer shock of it meant that it took a couple of seconds to realize there was a ten-year-old boy lying on the floor. With *my* camera in his hand.

The little brat had nicked it as he "helped" tidy up the splattered contents of my bag! From the millisecond he bent down to collect my stuff, he'd been hatching some scheme to get back behind closed doors and weasel around, with the hope that he could take a shot of something nasty, like a junior paparazzo.

Good. He deserved to get the fright of his life and faint.

If I didn't have so much respect for the little old lady sweetly lying there, or the fact that

Cormac's parents would go through the *roof*, I'd have been tempted to suggest we leave straightaway and lock The Weasel in there for the rest of the afternoon. . .

Nicking the nerk

Cormac had nicked it: nicked the word "nerk".

"Where did you hear that?" I asked, completely blown away that he'd used it in his act just now. I mean, I'd never heard anyone else say nerk before. Ever.

"Did Cormac see it on your computer, Sadie?" asked Letitia innocently.

"Ooh, has he been in your room without you telling us?" Hannah teased me, never letting a wind-up moment slip by.

Hannah was in a great (for that, read ditzy and cheeky) mood, boosted by the fact that her mum finally couldn't keep excusing Harry after the mess he got himself into yesterday. Still, I could do without her teasing me directly in front of Cormac like that. I chucked a daisy-chain at her head – I'm sure that taught her a lesson.

Cormac grinned shyly, kind of thrown at being part of our banter, as the four of us sat on

the grass, in the sunshine, in Highbury Fields.

People strolling by tended to stare, either because a) they were wondering why the red-headed boy was wearing a black suit and tie on a warm Sunday morning, or b) they'd caught him busking his comedy show, which had finished only a few minutes ago.

"Well, anyway – the 'nerk' thing. *You* said it yesterday, Sadie!" Cormac jumped in to answer, as he loosened the tight knot of black from round his white collar.

"Huh?"

I tried to work out when exactly I'd have brought up the subject of my brother, but couldn't think. The events of the day before were just a blur of weirdness.

"When you got hold of that vase, pulled out the roses, and poured the water over Harry, you were shouting, 'Wake up, you little nerk!!'," said Cormac, prompting my memory.

"Oh, yeah, *then*!" Hannah burst in. " 'Cause I was slapping his face, wasn't I? And you got *me* wet too!"

Y'know, if me and Hannah had gone on an up-to-date First Aid course, I bet they wouldn't advise you to throw water over an unconscious person, or slap them back into consciousness, for that matter. But I guess Harry came off pretty lightly, since both his sister and me would have happily *killed* him for what he'd tried to do. . .

"Whatever, you're *really* good, Cormac!" said Letitia, tilting her head to the side as she spoke, in a way that would make every single body language expert in the country yell, "SHE HAS A CRUSH THE SIZE OF A PLANET ON HIM!!" straight away. "You should get your family along – they'd be well impressed!"

Cormac shrugged, embarrassed and chuffed and quite possibly the only person in the universe who *wasn't* aware of Letitia's planet-sized crush, as he was too preoccupied with what he'd just done.

"I could hardly come out with that routine in front of my mum and dad and my brother Gerry – they'd go crazy if they knew what had happened with Mrs X!" he murmured, wincing a bit at the memory.

Mrs X . . . that's what he'd called the old lady in the coffin, to protect what shred of dignity she had left after Harry's little escapade.

"What about your other brother, Kyle?" I suggested. I was kind of intrigued to meet Kyle, having seen his style-explosion of a flat. I couldn't imagine him being a blend-into-the-background beige person after that. (Let's face it, a blend-into-the-background beige person wouldn't generally steal the keys of a hearse to transport a psychedelic '70s sofa.)

Cormac shrugged again. "Yeah . . . maybe. Maybe next time, if he's not away working on a shoot."

"What about some of your mates?" asked Hannah.

She'd talked about that on the way here – who Cormac's buddies might be, what sort of friends a teenage undertaker would have. . . It was her new fixation now that I'd put her out of her misery and described the wild and wacky home decoration in the flat above Dad's.

"Well, once I've completely nailed it, I'll ask them along," said Cormac, going into shrugging overtime.

It felt like he'd pretty much nailed it today. The three of us girls had stood dutifully in front of Cormac, who was perched nervously on his mini-stage (the wooden box he'd used last time). Slowly, slowly, people had come to nosey and gawp and wonder what was going on, and slowly, slowly, Cormac had started to relax.

Then pretty quickly, the milling audience of

Sunday morning strollers and dog walkers started to smile and laugh at what Cormac was coming out with. Not jokes exactly, just silly, rambling anecdotes, I guess you'd call them.

I was glad to see that he was sticking with the funeral director angle; it was his perfect gimmick, after all. He'd opened with some stuff comparing *his* work uniform (i.e. the sombre suit) to the "uniform" worn by boy band members (i.e. the neon cycling shorts Benny had persuaded my brother and the other boys to wear). You can guess where he went with that – i.e. all the way to Kennedy's exploding seams and Spiderman pants.

Luckily – or *unluckily*, since it was very funny – Sonny wasn't around to hear the boy-band rant. He was long gone by the time I'd got up this morning – off with Dad and the rest of S**** Rocks for their alternative bonding session. ("They've gone to some forest somewhere," Mum had said vaguely, as she'd changed Martha's nappy to the backdrop of some strident Wagner opera. "In Berkshire, I think. Or maybe it's in Hertfordshire . . . or did he say Essex?" My mum is nothing if not *vague*.)

As for the second section of his act, Cormac must have written it in a huge rush of inspiration yesterday, after the unadulterated Harry horror.

He spoke about it brilliantly, making everyone laugh (at Harry), but in a kind of bittersweet way:

"I reckon that I've identified two personality types that fancy psychologists haven't discovered yet: Useless Optimists, and Total Nerks. Take this lady that I know – Mrs X – who told the staff at her nursing home that she wanted an open casket when she died, so her friends and loved ones could see her and say their goodbyes. But sadly no one came. That's a Useless Optimist for you.

"Now, Harry is this kid who snuck into the funeral parlour, desperate to take a photo of a dead body. Yep, that makes him a Total Nerk straight away. But get this: he tries to take the photo with *someone else's* camera. How's that going to work? *How's* he going to download the shot without anyone knowing? What a Total Nerk. And then when he *does* catch a glimpse of Mrs X, he faints from shock. He's a Total Nerk times three!

"I tell you, being a Useless Optimist – even a *dead* one – is much better than being a nerk. . ."

As his words rattled through my head again, I knew I had to check something with Cormac.

"Is it really true that nobody came to see her?

The old lady, I mean?" I asked, wondering if he'd doctored the truth a little to make his routine more interesting.

"Not one person. Shame, isn't it?" Cormac replied.

We all went silent for a minute, mulling over how sad that was. To spend an amazing eighty-ish years on the planet, and have no one to show for it.

"Listen, I don't mean to come across like Harry, but . . . well . . . how did this Mrs X *look* exactly? With her being . . . *dead* and everything?" Letty suddenly asked, aiming her question more at me and Hannah than at Cormac.

Hannah and I stared at each other. Cormac stared at both of us, wondering, I suppose, how we were going to answer.

"She looked . . . well, quite *nice*, didn't she?" I said to Hannah.

"Yeah, she did!" Hannah nodded in total agreement.

"Well, that's just one of the great things funeral directors can do for a person," Cormac butted in, pleased – I was pretty sure – by our take on things. "I mean, it's a real privilege to make someone look as good as possible at the end, so the last goodbye is a nice memory for their families."

"If they bother showing up. . ." I murmured, thinking of poor Mrs X.

"Her hair was nice. Not mussed up or anything. And she had pretty make-up on. Who takes care of that stuff?" asked Hannah, intrigued.

"My mum, usually," said Cormac. "And Kyle used to do it too – that's where he got the idea to become a professional make-up artist."

Wow – that would be a *great* line to use when you were doing the make-up for stuck-up catwalk models ("I practised on dead people, you know. . .")

I noticed Hannah was frowning a little. What deep thoughts were running through her head? Maybe how weird death was? How strangely *ordinary* Mrs X had looked when we saw her? What Mrs X's real name was?

"Hey, I need new lipgloss. Anyone fancy a wander down the N1 shopping centre?"

Ah, Hannah, how horribly shallow she'd suddenly made herself sound.

I narrowed my eyes, shot her a look, and said, "Yeah, OK. Why not?"

Well, there's only a certain amount of death-talk an average girl can take in a day. . .

The order of bickering

"It looks nice!"

"No it doesn't!"

"It does! With those twinkly bits in it, it's all sort of . . . *shimmery*."

In order of bickering, that was Letitia, Hannah, and Letitia again.

Now, if I agreed with Hannah, and said this lipgloss wasn't nice, I would a) be telling the truth, but b) hurt Letty.

And if I agreed with Letty, I would a) be telling a lie, but b) hurt Hannah.

What a dilemma. Meanwhile, I was standing in the middle of Boots the Chemist, checking myself out in a make-up mirror, and thinking that I looked as if I'd smothered my mouth in glitter-glue.

"I sort of like it," I fibbed, to pacify Letty, "but then I think it's just too fancy – I'd never wear it."

There, that should satisfy Hannah too.

In the reflection of the mirror, I could see my friends standing either side of me, arms folded, plastic shopping bags dangling. Hannah had got herself a plain lipgloss and a couple of magazines, while Letitia had bought herself purple, over-the-knee socks. I'd kind of hoped to find myself a new comfort-blankie cardie from one of the high street stores in the N1 Shopping Centre, but I hadn't seen any. That I could *afford*, I mean.

So now the girls were trying to bully me into a cheap-ish fun purchase, so I could have a plastic bag to swish home with me too.

I just wished they'd suggested a bar of chocolate or a new pencil case ... something simple, that didn't involve me standing in the middle of this shop looking like a clown. I mean, someone from school could pass by and see me wearing this dumb sparkly gloop on my face, and I'd never live it—

"WHOAH!"

The boy's face looming into the mirror behind me looked familiar-ish, same as *my* face looked familiar-ish to *him*. What threw Sonny off was the glitter-glue mouth, I guess, and what threw me off about Sonny was his big black eye.

Well, I suppose it was more the colour of a

depressing rainbow at the moment: sage green, mustard yellow, stormy blue and bruised purple.

I grabbed a dusty, scrunched tissue out of my jeans pocket, gave my mouth a lightening wipe and spun round.

"What's going on? Did you ditch the idea of a boy band 'cause it's too naff? Have you joined an under-fourteens boxing club now?"

I felt a bit sick, to tell the truth, but Sonny seemed so freaked that I decided it was best to stay sarcastic so he knew where he was with me. If I'd been too nice and concerned, I worried he might freak out even more.

"No – it was Dad!" he said. Cue three girls' mouths immediately dropping open with a clang.

"*Dad* did that?" I asked, in a voice that could only be described as a squeak.

"Well, yeah, but—"

"D'you think *this* would work?" said Kennedy, shuffling over, his head bent as he studied a plastic tube in his hands. As he looked up, he gasped in surprise – partly 'cause he hadn't expected to see me and my two friends, and partly (though I didn't know it at the time) 'cause I had glitter-glue smeared halfway across my face.

Me, Hannah and Letty gasped right back.

The tennis ball-sized bruise on his neck looked

as if something large – a cow maybe – had given him a love bite.

"What's that?" I heard myself asking.

"Uh . . . Rimmel concealer, it says here," explained Kennedy, missing my point, and holding up the plastic squeezy bottle.

"It's OK – Dad didn't do that to Kennedy," Sonny stepped in, seeing what we were all staring at. "That was Ziggy."

I suddenly remembered what my brother was meant to have been doing this morning. Some band-bonding session somewhere, as organized by Dad.

So what had the bonding session involved, exactly? No-holds-barred wrestling? Bare-knuckle boxing? Or had it deteriorated into a general punch-up?

That didn't sound right; Dad was more of a peace, love and music kind of guy. He once told me that the only fight he'd ever had in his life was when he was fifteen, with a boy at school called Steven, who goaded Dad by repeatedly calling the Rolling Stones "complete [something very rude]".

"What were you all doing to each other?" I asked, frowning hard at both the boys, and wondering what the others looked like. Were Marcus, Hal and Ziggy as bashed up?

"Dad took us paintballing," Sonny explained. "We were in two teams in this forest, trying to blast each other."

"It was ace fun!" Kennedy grinned. "Kind of hurt though . . . when you got splatted with the paint pellets."

"That's 'cause we did it too close up," said Sonny. "The instructor warned us at the beginning how far apart we were supposed to be when we fired the paint guns."

"Only we forgot," Kennedy added, the bruise on his neck so livid it was practically *throbbing*.

"Where's Dad now?" I asked, wondering if he'd handed himself in at the police station, and was currently making a statement about his woeful failure to look after a bunch of kids in his care.

"He's dropping Mark, Alan and Gordon off at their houses," said Sonny, slipping into using his mates' real names. "We asked him to let us off here, so we could try and buy some cover-up stuff to hide the bruises."

The concealer, I suppose he meant.

"Did any of the others get hurt?" asked Hannah.

"Yeah. . ." said Kennedy, dopily laughing to himself at the memory of some paint-related injury or other.

"But Dad and the other lads, they've got bruises on their legs or bodies. Not their faces," said Sonny, checking his reflection out in the mirror again and acting all agitated.

Suddenly, I understood why.

"You're going to meet the record company tomorrow, aren't you?"

"Yeah – but are they going to sign us looking like *this*?" Sonny fretted.

I saw his point. As a shiny new junior pop band, the boys had to come across as squeaky clean and cutely handsome. Not like a bunch of trouble-making yob nutters.

"*I* know. Well, I *think* I know. . ." I told Sonny, as I rummaged in my pocket for my phone.

"Who are you calling?"

"Cormac," I told Hannah.

"Why?" asked Letty, suddenly all a-flutter.

"'Cause me and Kennedy are SO dead," groaned Sonny, slapping his hands over his face. . .

Half an hour later, Sonnt's hands were resting on his knees, and he was staring intently into a mirror surrounded by a frame of bright bulbs.

Kyle McConnell was meanwhile staring intently at my brother's bruise, which gave me a second to check him out. Kyle wasn't as flamboyant as his flat, that was for sure, but he still looked pretty interesting. He was tall and lanky, like Cormac, but with artfully tousled, mousey brown hair and a matching little goatee. He was dressed trendy-scruffy, if you see what I mean. The beat-up T-shirt with some Americana logo could have come from a charity shop, but more likely cost a zillion quid from a designer store.

"Head up a bit more," Kyle ordered, setting to work.

Hannah wasn't quite as busy. She'd kicked off her shoes and was lying flat out on the eye-swirling sofa, staring up at the black chandelier. Letitia was perched in the yellow plastic egg-shaped chair, giggling as Cormac demonstrated the fact that it could spin round. Kennedy was peering in the huge, gilt-edged mirror, admiring the disappearance of his look-a-like love bite.

"It's totally gone!" he gasped, tilting his chin this way and that, to catch alternative views of his neck.

"Well, like I said – this stuff is great," said Kyle, pointing the end of his make-up brush at a pot of foundation on the table. "It's got great coverage, but it looks really natural. Not like it's trowelled on."

Cormac's older brother hunched over my twin,

and briskly started covering up the bruise. He seemed to be enjoying the challenge and wasn't at all fazed by having five thirteen-year-olds invade his flat on a Sunday afternoon.

"But where can the boys buy that stuff?" I asked, leaning on the back of the gold-painted dining chair that Sonny was perched on.

"Oh, you can borrow it, no worries," Kyle said with a shrug. "I'll lend you a good make-up brush too."

"But I won't be able to put it on myself!" said Sonny, sounding alarmed, as his bruise started to vanish under brushstrokes of skintone. "We haven't started our classes in how to do stage make-up yet at my school. I mean, I've had other people do it to me, but—"

"*I'll* do it," I heard myself offering. "Before you go to your meeting tomorrow, I'll put your make-up on for you, yeah?"

"And me?" said Kennedy hopefully, spinning round from the big mirror.

"Sure," I said to old frying-pan face.

Hey, get me. I was nicer than I thought. I was going to be my brother's saviour, before the big signing tomorrow.

Sonny had better remember this and be grateful.

"By the way, Sadie – you want one of these for your face?" asked Kyle, handing me a sort of wet wipe from a packet on the table.

I dipped down enough to see my own reflection in the bulb-lit mirror. It was now that I spotted the smeared glitter-glue lipgloss. It had left a trail like a disco snail across my left cheek.

"Fnarrrrr!" snorted Sonny.

I was so glad that my misfortune had helped cheer him up. *Not*. . .

Chilly chips and name shame

"Ah, it would've been lovely to see you all dressed up, Sadie, love," Gran sighed, eyeing up my stripy T-shirt, tight black jeans and inevitably scruffy Converse trainers.

"I put *this* on!" I replied, pointing to the black sequinned Alice-band that was trying (and mostly failing) to hold my flop of hair back off my face.

Gran sighed again, wishing – not for the first time, I guessed – that I was more of a nice-skirt-and-pretty-top kind of granddaughter.

"Sushi?" said a bright, helpful voice by our sides.

Suddenly Gran – in her best navy pleated dress and pearls – looked like she was about to throw up on the expensive wooden tiled floor of this posh private members' club.

Just for a second, mind you, then she pulled herself together.

"No, thank you," she managed to say, holding

on to her dignity, as the waitress in front of her held out a silver platter piled high with slivers of raw fish.

The waitress, dressed in a sort of grey, Chinese-style linen suit, drifted off, and I went to Gran's rescue.

"Try one of these instead," I said, grabbing a dinky-sized portion of fish and chips (in its own fake "newspaper" wrapper) from the platter of a nearby waiter.

Gran took the fish and chips from me and studied it closely, and slightly disapprovingly. She might not have said it out loud, but I knew that in her head, she was tutting and muttering, "Whatever next?"

Overall, Gran wasn't too dazzled by the club where the record company had taken us for a post-contract signing party.

"Bit on the pokey side, isn't it?" she said, unimpressed with the roll call of celebs that Angie – the publicity girl from the record company – had told us came here.

"Don't see the point in champagne," she'd said sniffily, taking a cautious sip. "Why pay good money for something that gives you gas?"

And as for the sushi (the grown-up alternative to the kids' fish 'n' chips) . . . well, let's say she was probably twitching to take it back into the kitchen, get some oil in a frying pan, and cook it up properly.

Still, there had been a few things that got Gran's seal of approval this afternoon. Back at the record company boardroom, where all the parents signed the contracts on behalf of their sons, she'd been quite taken by the china cups and the selection of nice chocolate biscuits. And in the ladies' loos here at the club I'd caught her stroking the marble basins, then wondering aloud to Mum what cleaning products they used on the antique brass taps ("that's a lovely shine!").

"Mmm . . . could be hotter," Gran grumbled, nibbling at a skinny chip.

"OK, I'll get rid of it for you," I said, calling her bluff and holding out my hand.

"Oh, no – it's a sin to waste food," Gran replied, helping herself to a few more chips. "Ah, would you look at your brother? Isn't he handsome!"

Mr Handsome and his mates were currently being herded on to a tiny raised area of stage in the corner. The photographer who'd been snap-snap-snapping them for posterity – both back in the boardroom and for the last ten minutes as they mingled and chatted here with their

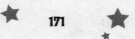

families – obviously hadn't had enough of their cheesy grinning faces yet.

As he stepped up on to the podium, I saw Sonny shoot me a questioning look.

I narrowed my eyes at him . . . then relaxed, giving him a quick thumbs-up. He didn't need a touch-up yet, but if he did, I had Kyle's pot of foundation and the make-up brush safely in my bag.

It had actually been kind of fun applying the make-up back at the house, before the taxi had arrived to whisk us off to the West End. When Sonny and Kennedy had started to get cheeky ("Going to be wearing your lipgloss that new way for the party?" "Across your face, he means!") I got instant revenge by threatening to do their make-up really *badly* – if they didn't behave themselves and say thank you in a very grovelling tone of voice.

As I'd swept and smoothed the make-up on, I'd even got excited about the idea of maybe following in Kyle's footprints one day and becoming a professional make-up artist. It would be great – just as long as I wasn't expected to grow a goatee too (beards just didn't suit me).

Or maybe I'd just do make-up for sweet old

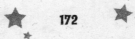

ladies like Mrs X, who needed to look nice for their last date with the world. . .

"Oh, dear – I'd better rescue your little sister," Gran muttered, placing the now-empty newspaper wrapper on a nearby table. "She's pulling that funny face she does when she's filling her nappy."

And off Gran strode, helpfully scooping Martha (dressed in her best baby party dress) from Mum's arms, and the nappy changing bag from off of Will's shoulders. I had a funny feeling that as well as her natural need to help out, Gran was looking for any excuse to go and admire the marble and brass of the club's bathroom again.

I thought for a second about going and joining Mum and Will, but then I saw them moving together to have a Martha-free hug, which was kind of sweet. And where was Dad? I glanced around the room, packed with proud parents, skittering kid brothers and sisters (there was a game of high-speed, under-the-tables chase going on), and highly-styled record company bods. The record company people reminded me of Kyle, dressed in slouchy, scruffy clothes that were probably hideously expensive.

And as an example, there was Angie the publicity person, in her tight, dark jeans, black

ballet pumps and a slash-necked, loose-knit top artfully falling off one shoulder. She was smiling in that blank way people do when they're bored to tears but don't dare show it. So what could be making her bored? Something coming out of Dad's mouth, it seemed.

I ambled over and linked my arm in his, my stripy green and pink T-shirt clashing horribly with his orange and white flowered Hawaiian shirt.

"Ah, there's my girl!" said Dad, giving my arm a squeeze. "I was just telling Angie how many CDs I've got in my collection!"

OK, so that answered my question. Just because this Angie girl worked in the music industry, didn't mean she would be thrilled to hear trainspotter-y facts and figures about Dad's record collection.

"So, are you as talented as your twin?" asked Angie, quickly turning her attention to me now that she'd spotted a lull in Dad's non-riveting conversation.

The answer, of course, was a flat no.

But I was feeling good today. I'd managed to fool Miss Cooper with Will's letter and appointment card this morning, and so kept my dignity, and I'd made Sonny and Kennedy look nearly as good as Kyle had done yesterday.

So I decided to be kinder on myself when I replied to Angie's question.

"I'm not into the kind of fluffy music the band play. I'm into grittier stuff, like the Foo Fighters and The Stone Roses."

Well done me. I'd managed to avoid mentioning the fact that I had zero talent, and I'd got a nod of approval for my musical choices from Angie at the same time.

"Our Sadie's got fantastic taste," Dad said proudly, making my heart flip with happiness. "You should see the track-listing on her iPod, it's—"

"Of course!" exclaimed Angie, her eyes suddenly alive and alert with possibilities. "You're Sadie! The one the band is named after!!

"Well, y—"

"Stuart! STUART!!" she suddenly called out to the busily snapping photographer. My arm was somehow disentangled from Dad's, and I found myself being steered through the throngs of chatting people and propelled towards the stage.

"What's happening?" I asked a fast-moving Angie in my best wibbly voice.

"Stuart!" Angie repeated at closer quarters, completely ignoring my question. "This is the *real* Sadie! The one the band is named after! We have to get a shot with her in the middle of all the boys!"

No, we don't, I thought, but my treacherous legs had already allowed themselves to be directed up on to the podium. All five of them – Sonny, Kennedy, Marcus, Hal and Ziggy – were grinning at me, which was ironic since I was dressed like a reasonable human and they were done up like a bunch of kippers.

"Just turn around and smile, Sadie, and if you lads could gather round, either side of her," said Stuart the photographer.

I tried to smile, I really did. But even my best friends know that my smile tends to look more like a sarcastic snarl. It's genetic – I can't help it.

"Let's have a better smile than that!" Stuart ordered cheerfully.

Yeah, like I was *really* in the mood. Everyone in this small, crowded room was now staring at me. Instantly, I imagined this photo popping up in a magazine if the band got famous: a magazine that people at school might read. Oh, the shame. . .

"C'mon, Sadie!!" Stuart ordered some more, as if that would jolly me into—

"WHAH!! HEEEHEEEE!!"

SNAP!

Great. Sonny had tickled me into laughing, and now there'd be a picture of me looking like a complete *loon*.

That was *seriously* not funny. . .

19

The secret cunning mind. . .

Things that are OK for rabbits to chew
- Apple or willow wood
- Pine firewood
- Cotton towels
- Hay
- Compressed alfalfa cubes

Things that are *not* OK for rabbits to chew
- Carpet (fibres are bad for them, apparently)
- Wood that might have been sprayed with pesticide
- Favourite cardies
- Camera cables that you are trying to attach to your computer so you can download photos

I'd just been online, checking a website dedicated to house rabbits so that I could read and understand why they chew so much.

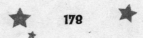

Apparently, this can be a sign of affection, in which case, that would make Clyde very, very affectionate indeed,

But then that didn't really match up with him trying extremely hard to nip me when I snatched the camera cable out of his mouth a few minutes ago.

But hey, we were buddies again. Clyde was cuddled in my lap, nibbling on my face-cloth (didn't think Mum would love me giving him one of our towels), while I gazed at a slide-show of all my recent photos.

PING!

"I've got mail!" I trilled to Clyde, who'd flinched a little at the sound zinging from the computer, but not enough to stop chewing his delicious face-cloth.

I let the slide-show roll on, as I opened my inbox and checked what had just landed in there.

Only me! the message – from Letitia – was headed. *Just saying hi –"*

Well, that was nice of her. It was so long since we'd seen each other . . . a whole twenty, maybe twenty-five minutes since I'd said bye on our way home from school this Tuesday afternoon. . .

– and I forgot to ask you something: can you find out the next time Cormac is doing one of his shows

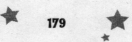

in Highbury Fields? I was going to ask him on Sunday, but I forgot. By the way, you know how he was spinning me around in that weird yellow chair in his brother's flat? Do you think that shows that he likes me? 'Cause I think that maybe it does, or maybe he was just being nice and –

PING!

Oh, hurray. Another email. Hopefully something more interesting than lovely Letty's less-than-lovely wittering about her Fantasy Boyfriend.

'YAY!!' was the heading on Hannah's email. *Hey! Great news – Dad was officially FURIOUS when he got back from his work trip today and found out what Harry had been up to on Saturday.*

Excellent! I was glad to hear that The Weasel was finally getting it in the neck.

I mean, Mum was mad for sure when it happened, but she went pretty quiet about it and I thought, NO!, she's going to let him get away with it, AGAIN! But she was obviously waiting for Dad to be around, and when I got in from school today I caught them giving Harry a HUGE talking-to about his behaviour. They even asked me to sit down with them, and have a think about a "suitable" way he might make it up to Cormac. THEY came up with this mad idea that Harry should write an apology

180

and send it into the funeral shop or whatever it's called, but I said absolutely NOT, 'cause Cormac would get into MEGA-trouble if his parents found out what had happened. Have you got any ideas what he could do or say to make it up, Sadie?

I didn't. But Cormac might. . .

Maybe I should forward this on to him, I mulled, thinking of Cormac, and how bad *he* felt about poor Mrs X. But how can you make something up to a dead person?

I swooshed the mouse up, meaning to hit the "forward" option, but I swooshed it a techno-step too far, and I found I'd accidentally brought myself back to the on-going slide-show.

Martha with the nasturtiums; Hannah pretending to drool outside that shop in Upper Street; Hannah pretending to be a fancy model and striking a pose in the middle of the pavement. . . Yikes! I forgot about the shot of the hearse passing by – delete!

Even with it gone, my stomach still lurched. It's just that the hearse had reminded me of something else. . . Harry had fainted before he got the chance to snap a photo of Mrs X, hadn't he?

I watched the slideshow with mounting horror.

OK, a sane photo.

OK, another sane photo.

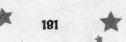

AAAAARRGGGHHH! A photo of a *dead* person!! Well, mostly of a shiny, pale wood coffin, with a little bit of the dead person showing inside. I blinked at the vision of Mrs X, and saw that the shot was sort of taken at an angle, as if Harry had pressed the shutter as he fell into his faint.

Delete!

I was still hyperventilating when someone hammered at my bedroom door, making me, Clyde and the face-cloth leap several centimetres into the air.

"Come in!" I squeaked.

A big black eye loomed into view, along with the rest of Sonny's face. He'd gone to school today minus his make-up, since it was back to normal lessons today (well, as normal as tap-dancing and voice projection can be).

"Just wanted to say, y'know, thanks for fixing me up yesterday," he said, letting his school bag slip off his shoulder and plonk on to the floor.

Ooh, that was fairly short and sweet for Sonny. I guess he was still a little nervous of me, knowing how grumpy I'd been about the tickling incident.

"S'OK," I said, trying to act cool © (copyright Will) and calm.

"Well, whatever . . . I owe you one!"

Sonny gave me a lop-sided smile and reversed out, dragging his bag with him.

PING!

That wasn't the computer this time; it was my brain, coming up with a slightly superb idea.

Sonny owed me one, and I suddenly knew how he could pay me back.

And I knew how Sonny could make it up to Cormac.

And I knew how Cormac could make it up to poor, sweet, dead Mrs X.

Wow, I had no idea I had such a cunning mind. . .

20

A very good deed indeed

"Do we get off here?" asked Letitia, all a-twitter.

She'd said that for the last ten bus stops.

It was as if the further we got from Highbury, the more she worried that we'd completely miss St Pancreas and Islington Cemetery, leave London behind and head out into Never-Never Land, never (ahem) to return. . .

"Yep, we're here," said Cormac, standing up to ring the bell. I knew we were being watched – by the driver and other passengers – as we trooped off the bus.

Maybe we *were* an odd sight. I mean, there was Cormac in his black suit, even though he wasn't officially working this Saturday; me, holding a glass jam jar crammed with cut-down carnations; Hannah, clutching a battery-operated bubble machine; Letitia, carrying the prettiest cake our combined pocket money could buy in M&S; Sonny, with his acoustic guitar strung across his back; and Harry, with a look of sheer fear on his face.

Well, who cared if people stared? The driver and passengers didn't have a clue, but we were all about to do someone a very good deed indeed – even if that someone was a bit too dead to appreciate it.

"Let's go," said Cormac, spotting a gap in the traffic and leading us to the gates of the cemetery. Well, he was used to coming here – only usually by hearse, and not the No. 134 bus.

"There're so many graves!" gasped Letitia dramatically, gawping at the row upon row of shiny headstones in front of us.

"Well, we'd be in the wrong place if there weren't," I pointed out, as – along with everyone else – I struggled to keep up with Cormac's long-legged stomp.

"Pity we weren't just going to the graveyard at the end of our garden," said Sonny with a grin.

Well, that would have been handy. But no one had been buried there for at least seventy years. (Did they put "FULL" signs up on cemeteries when they ran out of space?)

"Hannah. . ." came a plaintive voice from the back of our raggle-taggle crocodile. "Do I *have* to?"

"Yes, you HAVE to!" Hannah snapped, making

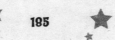

a grab for Harry's reluctant hand, in case of any escape bids.

"It's right over there!" announced Cormac. "The small marble one with the gold lettering."

We all left the path, and padded over neatly mown grass, stopping at this one particular gravestone.

"*'Maisie Alice Brown. . .'* that's Mrs X's real name?" I asked, looking at Cormac for confirmation that we were at the right spot.

"Yep. Mrs Maisie Alice Brown. *'Wife of Arthur Wilfred Brown, who died. . .'*" Cormac bent down a little to read the obviously older, more faded gold lettering on the lower half of the headstone. "*'. . .in 1960'*. Wow, she was a widow for a long time."

"But he's buried down there too, right?" Hannah checked.

"Yep," said Cormac with a nod. Right here, in this same plot!"

"Well, that's lovely. . . thinking of them together at last, under there!" Letitia murmured romantically.

Me and Sonny and Hannah all winced, with a less romantic idea of what was really going on under our feet.

OK, time to push grim reality out of heads and get happy – for Maisie Alice Brown's sake.

"Let's do it!" I said, placing the makeshift vase of flowers in front of Maisie's headstone. I dragged a tartan travel rug out of my back-pack and tossed it on the ground for us all to sit on.

A few minutes later, and we were attracting stares again, this time from an old couple on their way to pay a visit to a dead friend or family member. I don't know what attracted them first; the strumming of the guitar, or the drifting, popping cloud of bubbles, but whatever – it made them smile. And as smiles seem in short supply in graveyards, I thought that was pretty nice.

"Oh, I liked that one!" said Letty, through a mouthful of strawberry gateau.

Sonny had just finished singing something called "These Foolish Things".

"It's by George Gershwin," I told her, peeking at the top of Sonny's sheet music.

Mum had been brilliant this week; when I'd told her that I was researching music that Mrs X – Maisie – might have liked when she was a teenager, she'd not only reeled off a list of names that were big in the 1930s, but also tracked down some of the songs and sheet music in a dusty old cupboard in the music department at her school.

And of course Sonny had been brilliant too,

practising the tunes so he could help serenade Maisie at her very own "leaving" party today.

"Harry – it's *your* turn now," Hannah told her miserable-looking brother, who was fidgeting with a piece of paper in his hand.

Harry coughed, then reluctantly stood up, making eye contact with none of us.

"*Mmmummble, mummmummble, mummm—*"

"Louder!" Hannah told him sharply, nudging him in the knees with her elbow.

Harry coughed with embarrassment and started again.

"*Dear lady – I am sorry that I tried to take a photo of you when you were dead. It was very rude and bad and not a nice thing to do. I won't do it again. I apologize a lot. Harry. . .*"

He went to sit down, but Hannah shook her head at him.

"*And* the other thing you promised," she insisted.

Her brother rolled his eyes, but stayed where he was. Sonny began plucking notes on the guitar, and Harry reluctantly and tunelessly broke into a verse and chorus of "All Things Bright and Beautiful".

At the end of his punishment, we all gave Harry a round of applause, which made him blush even more. I plonked a slice of cake on a paper plate and roughly shoved it over to him. Typically, he didn't say thanks, and didn't seem so traumatized with embarrassment that he couldn't wolf it down.

"Cormac? *D'you* want another bit?" said Letitia, trying to force more party cake on her hero.

"No, I'm fine." He smiled as he leant back with his hands on the grass and his long legs awkwardly crossed in front of him. "You know something?"

I don't think any of us knew who this question was directed at, because his eyes were fixed on the bubbles drifting in multi-coloured twinkles above us.

"What?" asked Hannah, Letty and me in unison.

In the meantime, Sonny kept lazily strumming something or other, while Harry stuffed his face like he'd never seen food before.

"*This*," continued Cormac, "has been the nicest send-off I've ever seen!"

"Really?" I said, feeling myself pink-up at such a great compliment, since Maisie's "leaving" party had been all my idea.

"Uh-huh. I'd really love to tell Mum and Dad about it, but since we're here 'cause of all that breach-of-privacy stuff and everything. . ."

Cormac petered out. I guess he'd realized there was no point rubbing Harry's nose in it any more.

We all stayed silent for a while, maybe thinking warm thoughts about Maisie Alice Brown, or just watching the bubbles, or wondering who was going to eat that last slice of cake.

In the lull, my fingers got busy, absently plucking daisies and binding them together into a little garland. As I slotted another flower into another tiny stem, I sneaked a look up, first at Sonny and then at Harry.

Call me a mug, but I suddenly wondered if our annoying brothers (Hannah's and mine) weren't *so* bad after all. I mean, Harry might not have wanted to come and read out his apology or sing that hymn, but he'd done it, and helped make things right with both Cormac and Maisie Alice Brown.

As for Sonny. . .

Actually, what was Sonny *doing*? His genteel strumming had suddenly turned into something much, well, *noisier*.

"Sonny?" I interrupted, as he broke into a loud riff, his head practically banging in time.

"Oh!" said Sonny, giving me a black-eyed look of surprise. "Sorry – just messing about with a song I've been writing for Sadie Rocks!"

"Good grief – an eighty-three-year-old's leaving party is hardly the time or place for a pop song!" I told him off.

"Yeeeewwwwww. . . *Harry*!!" I suddenly heard Hannah gasp.

It wasn't the time to let one rip, either.

All of Maisie Alice Brown's mourners groaned as one, and scrabbled to their feet to get away from the deeply unpleasant whiff created by one mega-grinning ten-year-old.

"Guess that makes it a good time to go," said Cormac, brushing blades of grass and cake crumbs from his smart trousers.

So much for brothers turning over new leaves, I thought, quickly draping the daisy-chain garland on the headstone before grabbing up the travel rug.

"Bye bye, Maisie Alice Brown," I said softly, as our raggle-taggle crocodile padded back over the grass, crunched along the gravel path, and made our way out of the gate towards the busy road and the No. 134 bus stop

"Hey, what's that you're humming, Sadie?" Sonny suddenly asked me, as I studied the timetable to check on the next bus to take us in the direction of home.

Urgh – I'd been humming the irritatingly catchy new song that Sonny had just been

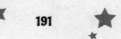

191

practising back at the graveside. How annoying to be caught doing that when I'd just told him off.

I quickly decided that the best thing would be to bite my lip and pretend I hadn't heard him.

"What's up with you?" Sonny asked. He was grinning, I could tell by the sound of his voice, even though I was deliberately blanking him.

"Nothing. I'm just great," I replied, poker-faced. "I'm absolutely awash with deep joy, or something like it."

More like deep annoyance, I thought to myself.

"'*Deep joy, or something like it. . .*'. Hey, that could be a great name for my new song!" announced Sonny.

Sigh. . .

I really hoped our bus came quickly, before I was tempted to hit my nerk of a twin brother over the head with his guitar.

What a beautiful, tuneless twang that would make. . .

Make friends with Karen McCombie!

"A funny and talented author"
Books Magazine

Once upon a time (OK, 1990),
Karen McCombie jumped in her beat-up car with
her boyfriend and a very bad-tempered cat,
leaving her native Scotland behind for the
bright lights of London and a desk at J17 magazine.
She's lived in London and acted like a
teenager every since. . .

Describe yourself in five words
Scottish, confident, shy, calm, ditzy.

How did you become a writer?
When I was eight, my teacher Miss Thomson told me I should write a book one day. I forgot about that for (lots of) years, then when I was working on teen magazines, I scribbled a few short stories for them and suddenly thought, "Hmmm, I'd love to try and write a book ... can I?" Luckily, I could. Yay!

Where do you write your books?
In the loft room at the top of our house. I work v. hard 'cause I only have a little bit of book-writing time - the rest of the day I'm making Playdough dinosaurs or pretend "cafés" with my little daughter, Milly.

What's the best thing about being a writer?
I feel like I'm a bit good at it. Especially when I get emails from girls who've read my books and tell me how they make them laugh, or make them enjoy reading, or have cheered them up when they've been going through a rough time. And that feels great.

✳ How long does it take you to finish a book?

It usually takes me a couple of months. I like to write lots and fast – it keeps me hooked on the story and totally in the mindset of the characters. Straight after I finish a book, I get very stupid and can't finish sentences; it's as if I've used up all the words in my head on the book!

✳ If you could be any character from a book, who would you be and why?

Probably Laura Ingalls Wilder, from the *Little House on the Prairie* series. It's a true-life story of a girl growing up in a nineteenth-century pioneering family in America. I'd love to be her just for the chance of seeing herds of buffalo roaming across vast prairies covered in wild flowers (i.e. before American got covered in malls, freeways and drive-in McDonalds!).

✳ What advice do you have for would-be author girls?

Keep EVERYTHING you write, even if you think it's pants. Come back to it and re-read it later and you might see a funny line, an interesting idea or a fun character you could pinch from it and use in future stories.

✳ What else do you get up to when you're not writing?

Reading, watching DVDs, eating crisps, patting cats and belly dancing!

Want to know more. . .?

Join Karen's club NOW!

For behind-the-scenes gossip on Karen's very own blog, fab competitions and photogalleries, become a fan member now on:

www.karenmccombie.com

P.S. Don't forget to send your bestest mate a groovy e-card once you've joined!

Karen says:

"It's sheeny and shiny, furry and er, funny in places! It's everything you could want from a website and a weeny bit more. . ."

Have you checked out the first *Sadie Rocks?* Book 1 is out now – don't miss it!

To: You
From: Stella
Subject: Stuff

Hi there!

You'd think it would be cool to live by the sea with all that sun, sand and ice cream. But, believe me, it's not such a breeze. I miss my best mate Frankie, my terror twin brothers drive me nuts and my mum and dad have gone daft over the country dump, sorry, "character cottage", that we're living in. I'm bored, and I'm fed up with being the new girl on the block.
Still, I quite fancy finding out more about the mysterious, deserted house in Sugar Bay. And what's with the bizarre old lady who feeds fairycakes to seagulls. . .?
Catch up with me (and my fat, psychic cat!) in the *Stella Etc.* series. LOL

stella
XXX

PS Here's a pic of me on a bad hair day (any day actually) with my mate Frankie. I'm the one on the right!

"Super-sweet and cool as an ice cream" *Mizz*

ALLY'S WORLD

"There's lots going on in my world – here's just some of what I have to deal with!!"

2 sisters – 1 bossy,
 1 bonkers
1 space-cadet brother
1 dad
0 mum
1 scruffy house in a nice place
 with a funny name
1 great view from my bedroom
2 dogs – Winslet and Rolf
 (don't even ask)
5 cats – 1's called Colin
Oh, and friends – lots.

"Now that you've finished this story, get into one of my adventures – there's heaps to choose from."

"Once you start reading you can't stop." *Mizz*

Heather thinks everyone in her family comes
from Planet Perfect. Everyone except her, that is.
Then Dad drops a bombshell, and the world
turns upside down...

Life's become surprising, exciting and just a little
bit mad – but is this topsy-turvy new family
somewhere Heather can fit in?

A scrumptious novel from best-selling author
Karen McCombie